Recipe for
Temptation

a Madewood Brothers novel

Gina Gordon

Entangled Publishing, LLC
2614 South Timberline Road
Suite 109
Fort Collins, CO 80525
Visit our website at www.entangledpublishing.com.

Brazen is an imprint of Entangled Publishing, LLC. For more information on our titles, visit www.brazenbooks.com.

Edited by Kate Brauning
Cover design by Heather Howland
Cover art from Shutterstock

Manufactured in the United States of America

First Edition August 2015

To the gut-wrenching, heart-palpitating, joyous journey to true love.

Chapter One

This was the life.

When Penn Foster awoke that morning, there was no tension in her body. No nauseous feeling in her stomach. All because she didn't have to see Cole Murphy—her sort-of boss, a pain in the ass, and one of the hottest men she'd ever encountered. Not for seven glorious days.

She lay on her back, her body stretched out on a lounge chair. The white resort towel spread under her was soft against her bare skin, and the bright midday sun shone down from a cloudless sky. A slight breeze wafted up to the pool area from the ocean and tickled the fine hairs on her arms. With a sigh, she settled against the folded-up towel under her neck, relaxed her shoulders, and soaked up the sun. She sneaked a peek down her body. Not that she'd be getting much sun. Not with the one-piece bathing suit she was forced to wear to cover the cherry blossom tattoo that spanned her entire left side. Her family didn't know about it.

Hell, they didn't know her at all. To them, she was the dutiful daughter and sister who always did what she was told. She'd been slapped with the boring, unadventurous wallflower stigma a long time ago, and they refused to see her as anything different. To this day, they couldn't understand why she hadn't settled down with a nice man and followed in her father's footsteps to become a teacher.

Because shaping the youth of tomorrow was God's honest work.

Which she believed in, but she wanted to do it in her own way. Like on the board of directors for the Vivian Madewood Foundation, a not-for-profit run by the Madewood brothers—her bosses. They used the foundation to raise funds for charitable causes aimed at helping children and youth across the city of Toronto in the name of their late foster mother, Vivian Madewood.

Fitting back into her wallflower persona was more and more difficult every time she saw her family, and she felt like she was leading a double life. But they just wouldn't understand the person she'd become.

When a shadow fell across her lounge chair, she peeked through one eye and saw a man standing with his back to her, blocking the sun.

"Do you mind moving over? I'm trying to get some sun," she muttered, closing her eye in annoyance.

The man complied immediately. She knew because she felt the heat against her skin again. But just as quickly as it had appeared, it disappeared. She turned her head and ripped off her sunglasses, then shielded her eyes with a hand pinned against her forehead.

The man had moved closer and was now turned toward

her, his shins almost touching the edge of her chair.

"Seriously, dude. Do you mi—"

Her shoulders shot up to her ears. She fisted one hand around the arm of the lounge chair and the other grasped her fruity drink in a death grip. Oh. My. God.

Cole Murphy.

Here.

In Hawaii.

On *her* vacation.

But why?

"How did I know you'd be lounging like a cat with your hand around a drink?" he drawled.

And with only a few words—not even a hello—he had managed to ruin the moment entirely.

"What are you doing here, Cole?" She sat up and placed her banana daiquiri on the small table beside her chair. She had *so* been looking forward to a week of perspective. To try and get a handle on her feelings for him before she returned home and cemented herself even further into the Madewood family business.

But with Cole here, in one fell swoop that plan had been squashed.

He straightened and clasped his hands at the small of his back. His eyes were hidden behind sexy wraparound sunglasses. "I'm on vacation."

Oh, *hell* no. He did not get to crash her family vacation.

"You don't vacation."

He hesitated, his body tensing for a brief moment.

She sat back in her lounger with a smug smile and enjoyed watching the small vein throb at his jaw. He was nervous. But she couldn't help her wandering gaze.

Damn, he was hot. He wore a white polo shirt and blue golf shorts. Tommy Hilfiger models had nothing on this guy. His hair, usually combed through, was haphazard, like he'd dried it with a towel and left it alone. She liked it. Made her think of her recurring daydream that had her running her hands through those brown strands and using them to guide his mouth to where she wanted it. Which was—All. Over. Her. Body.

Which absolutely was not going to happen.

She picked up the small white towel that sat on the table and dabbed her forehead. "Why are you really here?" He'd come all the way from his restaurant in Toronto, when usually nothing could make the man take a day off work. Not to mention they were two weeks away from launching his new project—the Madewood Boys and Girls Club. A project born out of guilt and anger because one of the students in his cooking program had been stabbed.

He puffed out his chest and crossed his arms over those hard pecs. "I'm here because…"

"Because?" Her fingers wrapped around the arms of the lounger, and her stomach tensed. Was he finally going to open up and tell her something, *anything*, that resembled a true emotion?

In an unsurprising move, he simply shook his head as if shaking off the rest of the sentence. "You need a partner to win the Foster Cup."

Be still my fucking heart.

He was here…for her.

To help her win the Foster Cup—the trophy given out to the winner of her father's ridiculous sporting challenge at the annual family vacation. That damn trophy still didn't have her name on it. Because she hadn't won—ever—not once in twenty years. She'd certainly bitched about it at work enough for him to remember. And boy, did she need his help. She'd already been partnered with her niece, Sara, for this morning's challenge.

And that was why she never won. All her siblings were happily paired off with their competitive, athletic spouses, and that left her to partner with one of the kids.

"Oh, I get it." She kicked her legs over the side of the lounger and slipped her feet into her beige, plastic flip-flops. When she looked up, he was eyeing her choice of footwear with a confused look. "You're here to help poor Penn. She's too spazzy to win the cup and needs help from a big, strong man."

His hands clenched. "You're not spazzy." He shrugged. "Maybe just unlucky?"

She snorted. "And you're going to be my good luck charm?"

A group of kids ran past them and jumped into the pool. Cole dodged out of the way and a splash narrowly missed him, but the ricochet of the water hitting the concrete had a welcome cooling effect against her hot skin.

She gathered up her sunscreen and water bottle and threw it in her cerulean-colored straw bag. She sighed and stood. "Look, Cole, I appreciate the offer, but there are rules, and you can't just show up and help me."

The Foster Cup had started off as innocent family fun, but became increasingly more competitive—and embarrassing for her—as the years went by.

"Let me help you."

If she had Cole on her team, she'd have a really good

chance at winning.

For the very first time.

Not to mention other intriguing possibilities.

"It's not that easy. My father…he's…"

She'd spent her entire adult life trying to be the opposite of her parents and her siblings. It might be selfish, but there was a method to her madness. Her loving family of six had been outwardly picture-perfect—mundane and boring. Inwardly, however, they were critical and judgmental.

As soon as she'd had the opportunity to fly the coop, she did, choosing not to follow in her father's footsteps but follow her own interests. Instead of teaching credentials, she earned degrees in both public relations and marketing. Her first job out of college was as an assistant copy editor for a marketing firm. But she'd ended up having an affair with her boss, and when she'd gotten promoted for no good reason other than her skills in pillow talk, she severed the relationship and found another job. There was no way she was going to build a career on her knees.

Which was why Cole being here wasn't such a great idea. The man had been her temptation for the last three years, and while she refused to let anything real happen, she could have told him every dirty thought she'd ever had about him and it wouldn't have made a difference. She loved teasing him because he was so cranky and easily embarrassed, and they'd slowly become friends, but the man was impenetrable. Completely immune to her charms.

Which was why there was no reason for him to be standing here next to the pool with her on vacation.

A squeal pierced her eardrums like an air raid. She knew exactly who that squeal belonged to. "Pennie!"

She froze. "Oh. Shit."

"Pennelope!"

"Go away," she ordered Cole through gritted teeth. "Go before they see you." She pulled at his bicep and yanked him, but she pulled too hard. Their bodies slammed together, rubbing his rock-hard abs against her. His biceps bulged under her grip. And the way he smelled—like the very best spices in his kitchen mixed with the perfect man-smell that was unique only to Cole.

He looked over her head and murmured, "Who's Barbie and Ken?" His breath was a warm sensation across her skin.

She shivered and swayed even closer, but then they were swarmed, her sister-in-law, Cathy, pulling her out of his arms. Which she greatly appreciated, because she didn't think she'd be able to do it herself.

Cathy squealed and nattered on with excitement. "Oh, my, God. It's Cole Murphy." She grabbed at his bicep, an inappropriate gleam in her eye.

"What is Cole Murphy doing here, Pennie?" One of Cathy's eyebrows quirked up as she crossed her arms over her chest, waiting for a response.

How the hell was she going to explain this?

She turned to Cole and took a deep breath. No getting out of introductions now. "Cole, this is my sister-in-law, Cathy." She pointed to her right. "And my brother, Ian."

Ian took a few steps forward and held out his hand. His brown hair and swim trunks were soaked. Cole shook it with a tentative smile. "Cath, I think you should let the poor man breathe." He grabbed his wife's arm and pulled her away from Cole.

"And those are my sisters-in-law, Beth and Christine,

and my brothers, Dave and Pete."

Beth eyed Cole with the same curiosity as Cathy. Dave stared him down, most likely sizing up his strength. Pete and Christine were just…smirking. They were the only ones in her family who knew how she felt about Cole. Well, a watered-down version of how she felt, but they knew there was *something* there.

"Pennie, this is so exciting." Cathy's excitement had her blond hair, gathered in a high ponytail, swinging like a pendulum. "You didn't tell us you were bringing a celebrity on vacation!" She gleefully pointed her long index finger, made even longer by her cat manicure, at Cole.

This *was* a celebrity sighting for Cathy. Cole and his brothers were infamous back home in Toronto and more than occasionally headlined the newspapers and gossip sites. Their mother, a do-gooder socialite, had adopted them, and by association, they'd been thrust into the limelight, which she knew Cole despised.

Just then, two little whirlwinds broke through the crowd of adults, bubbling with excitement, though one stayed a few paces back from Cole. Her nephew was as shy as her niece was outgoing.

"This is my niece, Sara, and that little monkey hiding behind Ian is Andy, my nephew."

Sara tugged on Cole's shirt. "Who are you?" Her silky, blond hair blew across her face in the gentle Hawaiian breeze.

When Penn glanced up at Cole, she expected to see terror on his face, but instead she saw an expression that was all too rare.

Happiness.

It lit up his entire face. His cheeks flushed, and she knew if he didn't have his sunglasses on, his eyes would be sparkling in the sunlight.

"I'm…your aunt's friend."

Friend. Not coworker?

Andy's shyness didn't last long. The moment Sara touched Cole, Andy raced over. "Do you like Legos? I like to play with Legos. Maybe we can build a castle or a fortress."

Penn smiled, unable to contain her own joy. Despite unleashing the crazy that was the Foster clan, she had inadvertently made him happy. And in the end, that's all she'd ever wanted for him. He deserved happiness in his life. Something that, over the last three years, she'd watched him struggle to find but never quite keep.

Cole was the most negative person she'd ever encountered. Considering his upbringing in the foster care system, it was warranted, but for the last three years she'd been trying her damnedest to get him out of this life-long funk, this cloud of pessimism she'd bet he'd had since childhood.

If the Boys and Girls Club didn't work out, he'd be devastated. Which was why she was going to do everything in her power to make it a success. As the marketing and publicity director for the Madewood Empire, it was her job. As Cole's friend, it was her duty.

But on a big picture level, it was necessary.

A spot on the board of directors for the Vivian Madewood Foundation was now vacant, and it was the perfect opportunity to take her career to the next level. Cole's late foster mother's best friend, Gloria, had relinquished her position, and Penn was the perfect replacement. She had every intention of rocking the Madewood boys' socks off and lobbying for it once the club was up and running.

Cole looked down at Sara with a warm smile. Penn's heart clenched in happiness at the soft expression. "I came to help your *Aunt Pennie* win the cup."

She sneered at the use of her nickname. She wished he'd never heard it.

"Oh no you don't, mister. You can't play," Cathy scolded with a wag of her finger.

"Hell, no." Beth was a little more adamant, but they were both right. "Only significant others." Beth pursed her lips in an I-told-you-so gesture.

Her sisters-in-law were right. But maybe she could get her father to change the rules. For once, give her a chance to win.

"Are you significant others?" Christine grinned from the sidelines, her pregnant belly just becoming noticeable under her clothing.

Hey, ground. This would be the perfect time for you to open up and swallow me whole.

Before she had time to look over at Cole and gauge his reaction to that question, Ian changed the subject.

"We're due to meet our parents on the beach." He pushed forward. "You know the Sergeant will want to weigh in on your..." He raised an eyebrow. "*Friend.*"

The Sergeant was the nickname her brothers had given their father when they were kids. He knew nothing about it, of course.

Ian herded the family away, and they followed behind, a twinge of revenge settling in Penn's stomach. Oh, yeah. She'd seen Cole in action many times: hockey, baseball, his smoking body on a treadmill. She knew he'd wipe them all off the map. And since he was already here and willing, she had to do whatever it took to get him on her team.

"Are you sure about this?" She looked up, biting her bottom lip. "What about the club?"

He shrugged. "It won't fall apart in a week."

Her heart leaped. If there was one thing Cole Murphy was not, it was blasé. But this man walking beside her had somehow shown up when she'd least expected it, but needed him the most.

She pulled him to a stop and hugged him. He was stiff at first, and she should have known better than to show any sign of affection, but she just couldn't help herself. He might have just sealed the deal for her to win her first Foster Cup.

The longer she held him tight, the more relaxed his body became. He even swept his arms up and wrapped them around her before settling at her lower back.

Without releasing her grip, she tipped her head back and looked up at him.

He gazed down at her with a serious expression and said, "Pennie? Really?"

She released him and smacked her hand against his stomach. "Shut up, Murphy."

He laughed, and in an unusual show of affection, rested his arm over her shoulders, then pulled her into his body. With a laugh, he said, "Watching you squirm for an entire week is going to be entertaining."

They walked through the pool area, then across the patio to the beach where her parents and family were waiting. Penn relished the feel of his warm, hard body pressed against hers.

She'd wanted this man for three years. Even though she knew better, even though wanting him was the best way to erase every inch of professional success she'd gained for herself along the way.

Shameless flirting had always been her saving grace because she knew deep down he'd never flirt back. But now he was here, and that had to mean something.

She'd come to this island for some perspective. She had a cup to win and a promotion to clinch. Nothing was going to stand in her way. But then Cole lowered his arm and tightened his grip on her body, his fingers massaging her hip.

She stifled a whimper.

Turns out even her best laid plans were no match for Cole Murphy.

Chapter Two

How did he get himself into this mess?

Yesterday, Cole had been in his kitchen at Bistro, doing his executive chef thing, and today he was on a beach in Hawaii, meeting Penn's entire family. And competing in some bizarre family sporting ritual.

Thanks to his brothers' coaxing—more like threats—he was also on vacation. Jack Vaughn, Neil Harrison, and Finn O'Reilly had cornered him in the stock room. They were afraid he was going to snap before the launch of his new project—the Madewood Boys and Girls Club.

But he had to admit, the moment that little girl had tugged on his arm, he'd been mesmerized. By this totally normal, everyday family.

Until he was taken in by Vivian, to Cole a family was just the people you were obligated to, the ones who always let you down. Vivian Madewood had given him a real family when he'd least expected it. His adopted family was great—

the best. But they were hardly normal.

Penn walked beside him as they meandered along the winding walkway that outlined three humungous pools. He'd never seen her so complacent. His strong, independent, mouthy Penn. The only recognizable thing about her was the oversized sunglasses perched on her nose. Otherwise, she was almost unrecognizable in a one-piece bathing suit with a plain blue straw bag slung over her shoulder. What happened to her designer clothes and expensive accessories? And where were the high heels? If she was going to wear flip-flops all week, his neck was going to be sore from looking down all the time. And she was completely covering up his favorite asset—her awesome cleavage. Not to mention hiding the cherry blossom tattoo he'd found out about a year ago at Sterling's bachelorette party, when he'd mistakenly ogled her half-naked boudoir photos.

He'd never minded her flirting with him. It was just her personality. But seeing those photos had jarred something in him to life, and ever since then, her teasing had almost pushed him over the edge.

The Penn he'd come to know over the last three years liked to emphasize her cleavage, and seeing her in a skimpy bikini was what he'd started fantasizing about as soon as he'd settled into his seat on the plane.

Not that her in a bikini was why he'd come here.

"Why are you looking at me like that?" She dropped her gaze to her body. "Is there something wrong with what I'm wearing?"

"Not at all." He lifted his hands in defense. "I just... Well, it's just not the type of bathing suit I pictured you favoring." When his hand lowered to his side, he grazed her hand, sending a singe of sensation right to his cock.

"You've pictured me in a bathing suit?"

Shit! Stop talking. Just shut up.

He needed to change the subject. To anything that wouldn't lead to him fantasizing about her naked, or in skimpy clothes, or better yet, at all. A sexual tryst was the last thing he wanted in the public domain. Cole had done his best to steer clear of the gossip columns, leaving the spotlight to his brothers, Neil and Jack.

He cleared his throat. "Is there a reason why you're hiding your tattoo?"

This was something he needed to get to the bottom of. It wasn't just her outfit that had him confused. It was her whole personality. While interacting with her family, she had shrunk into herself. She'd become nervous. The complete opposite of the Penn he knew.

The Penn who showed up every day to work was confident and competent in sky-high heels and pencil skirts showing off legs he couldn't help but imagine went all the way up to that spot he'd been dying to sink his—

"Who said I'm hiding it?" she muttered. She threaded her arm through his as they walked onto the beach. "Let's just focus on getting my father to agree to let you stay."

Penn had been there for him more times than he could count. Which was why he was here, instead of back home, working out the last-minute details for the club.

It was an initiative born out of anger. And Cole sure as shit had been mad when he'd found out one of the teens in the Cooking For the Future program—the culinary program established by his foster mother, Vivian Madewood—had died. Something inside him had snapped. Admittedly, his initial approach with his brothers might not have been the best idea, or the most professional. He'd shown up half-cocked, guns blazing, with a business plan written on lined paper, his words scrawled across the white space in a serial killer-esque code.

But that kid's death had hit too close to home, brought back too many memories from his own tormented childhood for him to waste any time. At that moment, he'd vowed to do whatever it took to keep another kid from ending up with his same sad fate.

Up ahead, he recognized the men he'd met five minutes earlier. But those men now wore bright yellow T-shirts. Matching T-shirts. Along with the rest of the family.

FOSTER FAMILY FUN-CATION

Christ. Were they for real?

But the closer they got to the group, the more he realized he was being eyeballed. By an older man who must be her father. He stood with his feet shoulder-width apart and his arms clasped behind his back. Military? He looked way too rigid to be an accountant or a salesman. He stood beside an attractive middle-aged woman—presumably Penn's mother—who held a tiny baby in her arms.

Why didn't Cole know what her father did for a living? Why didn't he know anything about any of her family? They'd spent so much time together, though most of the time every word that came out of her mouth was arguing with him.

Cole hadn't had much experience with the fathers of the women he'd dated. Mostly because he hadn't dated anyone long enough. This was all new. This was all terrifying.

He wasn't the man anyone brought home to meet the

parents. He was the son of a prostitute, who held no shame in bringing home her tricks. His father— He had no idea who that might even be. He'd often had to steal just to eat, and the cherry on top of his childhood had been the day he was removed from his dirty, unkempt apartment and placed into foster care.

They walked up to her parents, and she squeezed his arm. And just like that, with her simple touch, his uneasiness disappeared.

"Cole, this is my father, Harold Foster. Dad, Cole Murphy." The older man extended his hand, and Cole grasped the surprisingly solid grip. His salt and pepper hair was cut short, probably with the second highest setting to a shaver. Definitely armed forces.

"Pleasure to meet you, sir."

"This my mother, Margot." Penn lifted onto her toes and peeked into the pink blanket. "And this is baby Hannah, Dave and Beth's little one."

Cole straightened his shoulders and held out his hand. "It's a pleasure to meet you, Mrs. Foster." He hoped no one would notice he'd glossed over the baby. He wasn't much for the goo-goo, ga-ga. "Great T-shirts, sir. Very creative," he ventured, casting about for something to say.

"Not really, guy," her brother, Dave, said from his left.

Ian helped Andy pack down some sand into a pail, then flip it over. "Dad, you promised you'd never make us wear these lame T-shirts ever again."

"Not after the copycat fiasco of 2009," Beth put in.

Cole leaned down and whispered in Penn's ear. "The copycat fiasco?"

She shook her head and rolled her eyes. "I'll tell you

later."

"Nonsense. How else are guests supposed to know who we are and why we're here?" her father said.

Ian didn't look too pleased about the Brady Bunch routine. "They're not. That's the beauty of this world. Not everyone has to know your business."

"Beth, dear"—Margot motioned to a pile of bags on the beach—"could you please grab Pennie and Cole a couple of shirts?"

He couldn't stop the laugh that escaped at hearing her nickname, but he coughed when her hand flew into his stomach.

"I hear you want to compete." The man didn't beat around the bush.

Penn tensed at his side. "Yes, Dad. I was wondering if… well, would it be possible if…"

Who was this woman, and what had she done with Penn Foster?

"Then you two are dating?" her mother asked.

The question plunged them into silence. An awkward, tense silence that made it feel like Cole wasn't the only one waiting for an answer. So was the entire beach.

"No, Mom." Penn squirmed beside him. "We're just friends."

He let out a shaky breath, careful not to make his nervousness so visible. He refused to show any signs of weakness.

"Just friends," he confirmed, straightening his shoulders and lifting his chin. "From what I gather, your other children have an unfair advantage." Penn dug her nails into his forearm. He repressed the need to flinch. "I think it's about time Penn had some equal footing."

Her mother wore a pleased little smile and craned her neck to look into her husband's eyes.

"This is a historic year for the Foster Cup," her father boasted. "The twentieth anniversary."

Penn deflated beside him. "Yes, sir. I understand."

Why was she giving up so easily? He didn't plan on going so quietly.

Harold crossed his arms over his chest and eyed Cole. He met his stare with conviction, with every shred of pride he could muster.

Harold nodded. "Then maybe the rules can be bent, just this once."

Penn squeaked beside him and threaded her fingers through his.

"Dad, no!" Beth spat just as she threw their T-shirts, one of them walloping Penn in the face.

"Now, Beth." Harold pulled her into his side and rubbed her bicep with affection. "Mr. Murphy has traveled all this way. I should at least give him a chance to prove if he's worthy of participating."

A smirk curved at the side of Beth's face. Shit, this wasn't going to be so easy.

He looked around at the rest of her family who'd kept themselves occupied during the introduction, but he knew they were watching out of the corner of their eyes.

"Is that why you summoned us here, Dad?" Cathy asked with a frustrated sigh. "Do you have some kind of challenge set up for us?" Her impatience was a tad annoying, considering she was well beyond her teens. Penn had rarely spoken of her family, but it didn't take a rocket scientist to peg them all at first glance.

Cole leaned down and whispered in Penn's ear, "Is your dad ex-military?"

She shook her head. "Retired high school gym teacher."

He laughed. This all definitely made more sense now.

Her father walked over to stand in the middle of the group. "Welcome to the Foster Family Fun-cation!" he boomed.

Penn groaned beside Cole. Despite the insider peek he was about to get into her family dynamic, he felt that groan right between his legs.

"We are here in this perfect setting to celebrate the twentieth anniversary of the Foster Cup. As you know," her father continued, "the annual challenge consists of several challenges. The team with the most wins gets the cup."

"We're ready!" Beth pumped her fist.

"See what I'm dealing with?" Penn muttered under her breath.

"Before we get started, we need to figure out if our guest is capable of running with the Fosters."

"This is pointless." Dave sighed. "Penn isn't going to win anyway."

"She just might." Cole directed his smile at Beth from across the group and winked. "Now that *I'm* here."

Penn looked up; her eyes sparkled with happiness. *There.* That look was exactly what he'd wanted to see. And surprisingly, exactly what he'd needed to feel.

The Hawaiian sun beat down on his head and tingled across his arms, legs, and neck. Yet that wasn't the reason for the warm, tingly feeling that spread through his body, unfamiliar but so welcome.

He shook it off. He needed to focus on what was

important. Namely, winning this trophy for Penn. She'd been by his side the entire time he'd been planning and getting the club off the ground. Showing up here in paradise to show off his athletic skills was the least he could do.

Her father clapped to get everyone's attention and waved his arm toward the water. The little kids jumped up and down, screaming, then darted across the beach to where three kayaks lay on the shoreline.

Why did Cole feel like he was being led toward a firing squad, like he was walking the green mile?

But when Penn grabbed his hand and squeezed, her hand lingering for only a moment before she pulled it away, something other than nervousness hung in the air. Something more potent, more priceless.

Since the very first day he'd met Penn, he'd felt an unspoken connection that ebbed and flowed between them, and no matter how hard he'd tried to deny it, that connection could only be described with one word.

Mine.

As if it was instinctive—an overwhelming urge to claim her that he'd pushed aside for three long years.

Maybe that wasn't in the cards. But he sure as shit could win this challenge.

It was time for a Murphy to kick some Foster ass.

Penn's mother, who still held baby Hannah, had joined the kids by the kayaks but away from the rest of the group.

Harold stood out from the crowd and addressed the family. "The object of this challenge is a race to the first buoy." He pointed at the water. "I had originally planned on this being a team challenge, but the situation has changed. Gentlemen will participate, ladies, you will sit this one out.

Mr. Murphy?"

Cole tensed and straightened. Just the sound of Harold's voice brought him right back to grade school.

"If you are the first to capture a flag from the buoy, pin it to your T-shirt, then kayak back to the beach, then you can stay and compete as Pennie's partner."

"Is this for real?" Cole looked down at Penn, who was shaking her head.

"Oh, yeah. My father probably paid a premium to have hotel staff help set up the challenges."

"This is a bit extreme." Harold Foster was hardcore.

She rolled her eyes. "You have no idea."

Penn squared her body in front of him and reached out to grasp his hands. "Please, Cole. I need this. If you can set the tone and win this challenge, you will have made the last twenty years of humiliation and loss so worth it."

Given the chance, he'd gladly spare her from humiliation and loss for as long as she'd let him.

"Don't worry, babe." He winked. "I got this." He strode to the kayaks where her father stood holding an air horn. Pete had decided to sit this one out. Instead, he sat beside his wife with a wide smile, his hand stroking her baby bump.

At the starting line, there was no sense of camaraderie. Even at ten years old when he'd first met Finn, he'd known right away they had a special relationship. And five years later, when he'd only been living with Vivian for a few short weeks, he'd known Neil was a true brother. But not these guys. These guys weren't here to be friends. They were in it to win it.

"No hard feelings." Dave leaned over and held out his hand. "But I'm going hard. Beth tends to get a little —"

"Crazy." Ian finished his sentence. He pulled down his sunglasses enough to look over the tops. "I've never met a more competitive person in my life. She can't even lose at board games without going bananas."

"Well, boys. I'm going hard, too." Cole turned his head and focused on the water in front of them. "It's about time Penn had her name on that trophy." And he wasn't leaving this island until she did.

"Come on, baby. You got this," Beth yelled from behind them.

"Yeah, Cole," Penn yelled, her voice cracking. "We're going to win."

He looked over his shoulder, and Penn made a face. They were both so out of their element. If they managed to pull this off, it would be a damn miracle.

The air horn went off with a wail. Cole darted to the kayak on the right. Without slowing, he pushed it down the beach into the water. When he was thigh deep, he jumped in, balancing himself with the paddle. The buoy was about two hundred feet out. Dave came up beside him, and seconds later, Ian was at his opposite side.

They all began to paddle at the same time.

Despite Cole's wraparounds, the glare from the sun off the water was blinding. He paddled like mad, alternating sides. He had a slight lead, but Dave and Ian were a stroke behind.

In the background, the hoots and hollers of their significant others carried over the water. He knew Penn would be doing a good job of holding her own. But trying to hold her own was so not the Penn he knew. The Penn he knew would have her elbows up, pushing her sisters-in-law out of the way, one hard jab at a time.

He shook his head, focusing firmly on the buoy. He was just a few strokes away. Dave's kayak rammed into his, but Cole held his ground, using his paddle to swerve his vessel to the right. He squeezed between Dave and the buoy and grabbed the red flag with his left hand.

He paddled around and beelined it back to the beach after quickly clipping the flag to his T-shirt. Dave was right behind him. When they got to shallow water, Cole leaped out and dragged the kayak to shore.

Penn stood off to the side, biting her fingernails, while Cathy and Beth cheered on their husbands. She had nothing to be nervous about. He was going to win this thing. For her.

He felt Dave right behind him. One trip, one fumble, and it would be all over.

Dave muscled his way beside him, but he shoved him with his left shoulder. They battled for the lead, and by some miracle, Dave tripped trying to take him down. Cole charged ahead, reaching Harold with his flag securely pinned to his shirt. He flung his arms in the air.

His exhilaration was cut short when Penn launched herself into his arms and wrapped her legs around his waist, squeezing him with a strength he'd never guess she was capable of.

He took care to hold her, despite the overwhelming urge to lower his hands and cup her tight, round ass. Instead, he brought one hand up to cradle the back of her head.

He heard her short breaths in his ear, felt the pounding of her heart against his own chest, smelled her citrus-y shampoo, and groaned when he registered the warmth of her flesh against his stomach.

He felt it all, every nuance of her body language, and in two seconds, she was going to feel *his* pressed against her ass.

He grabbed her under the arms and pried her away from his body. This was not the time to discover there might be a new layer to their relationship—one that pushed the boundaries he'd been so intent on keeping in line. And it definitely wasn't the place, since they were in public.

As if recognizing they'd crossed a line, she stepped back once she'd steadied herself on the sand. Instead of looking at her, he locked his gaze on the sand below.

"Fair is fair." Penn's father approached and clapped him on the shoulder. "Your appearance this year might very well have changed the dynamic of the games, Mr. Murphy."

Not just of the games. But of Cole's relationship with Penn. By the end of the week, they were either going to be best friends—closer than ever—or he'd lose the only friend he might one day trust with the truth.

Chapter Three

Penn stared at her reflection in her hotel room mirror, trying her best to swipe a gloss applicator across her lips. But it was a lost cause. Her hundred-watt smile made it virtually impossible to put it on smoothly.

She didn't look any different. But inside, she felt vindicated. *Suck on that, Foster clan.*

She shook her head. No reason to get cocky. She hadn't won anything yet. Today was just a friendly challenge. A challenge where Cole had handed her brothers their asses. And the look on Beth's face when Dave lost—oh my God. Penn sighed with contentedness. Oh, man, she was never going to get that pissed-off expression out of her head.

But if today was a foreshadowing of events to come, she was totally going to win. She felt it in her bones. And it was all because of the hulking man who now stood in the doorway to her bathroom.

She'd felt his presence even before his reflection

appeared in the mirror. He just had that effect on her. As if they were connected on a level more intimate and all-consuming, more potent, than any star-crossed lovers.

Not that they were in love or anything.

"Now, that is the smile of someone who's gloating."

She ran the tip of her finger under her left eye, wiping away a few lines of black mascara that had transferred from her eyelashes, then turned. "And I have you to thank for it."

The moment her eyes landed on him, her stomach tightened in excitement.

He had rested his forearm on the doorjamb and leaned in, the white linen of his button-down shirt lifting on one side, exposing his tanned skin and the line of hair that ran down his chest and disappeared into his shorts. And as she was checking him out, he was doing the same. His gaze roamed over her body, taking in the curves she'd squeezed into a red sundress.

The look in his eyes was disarming. She'd also seen it when she'd launched herself at him after his win today.

Desire.

It flickered in his gaze, and it took everything she had not to pull him down on top of her right then and there. She'd been there, done that, and suffered the effects of her bad decisions.

So, she did what she did best when it came to Cole Murphy. It was time for a little tease.

"It's a little hot in here, right?" She slipped off the tiny sweater she'd put over her sundress, exposing the body part she knew he couldn't take his eyes off. The minidress had a built-in bra so her breasts were pushed together high, giving her perfect cleavage. And when she bent over, the hem of her dress lifted, giving him an excellent view of where thigh met ass cheek.

She looked in the mirror and caught his eyes. Oh, yeah. He liked it. That jawbone was twitching a mile a minute, and she saw his hand make a fist and his forearm clench where it rested on the doorframe.

She turned, rested her bum on the bathroom vanity, and asked, "Did you have a good time with Dave and Ian?"

It took him a minute to gather himself and to stop staring at her body, but eventually, he jerked a nod. "They're good guys."

"You know the reason they invited you for a drink was because Dave didn't want to go back to his room quite yet." She didn't blame Dave one bit. Over the last ten years, she had learned that Beth was even more competitive than her brother, and she made no effort to conceal that behavior. In fact, Penn had a real suspicion it was the reason Dave fell in love with her in the first place.

"I got that after a few minutes." Cole laughed. "It took some coaxing to get him to leave the bar." He pushed off the doorjamb and walked into the bathroom, past the glass shower stall, and sat on the edge of the Jacuzzi tub. Resting his hands casually on either side of his body, he said, "Your whole family, even the in-laws, are…intense."

She scoffed. "That's a nice way of putting it." She let herself relax. "Needless to say, family game night was, and still remains, a nightmare."

She turned back to the mirror and picked up her gloss before swiping the applicator across her lips. "Was your family competitive?" she asked.

He gave her his best are-you-kidding-me look. "Have

you *met* Neil Harrison?"

She knew all about his brothers. She worked with them every day. He didn't have to school her in their behaviors and quirks. "Not your Madewood family, your real family." *Shit, Penn. Could you be more insensitive?* "I mean…your biological parents."

His face instantly grew serious. "The Madewoods *are* my real family."

She'd hit a nerve. But he wasn't getting off that easy.

She gazed at him in the mirror, her foot tapping on the tile. When her eyebrow quirked up in a challenge, he conceded. She got a mumbled answer.

"I don't remember."

She was calling bullshit on that. But she wasn't going to pry. At least, not yet.

They were off to family dinner, which, for a change, she was actually looking forward to. Not just because Cole would be by her side. This time, she could finally show them her true competitive nature. She now had the means to put her money where her mouth was.

"When you won that challenge, it was the best I've felt around my family in a really long—" She stopped and looked up to face him. "Ever."

Thirty years old, and it had taken this long for her to truly feel like a winner. And she hadn't even won the race herself.

She took a deep breath. Now was not the time to get mopey. She had plenty of time this week to prove she could win on her own. And with Cole here to support her, she knew she could do it.

Silence grew between them until he stood and wandered

over to the vanity.

He fiddled with one of her eyeliners sitting on the counter, twirling the stick, his hand getting closer and closer to where hers rested on the vanity. Personal space had always been an issue for Cole. Until he set foot on this island. Maybe harmless flirting didn't mean the same thing in a tropical paradise.

His fingers brushed the side of her hand and she gasped. Then, intentionally, he stroked the top of her hand. "Your skin is so soft." His was hard, roughened from the years spent with his hands preparing food.

He turned and reached out, his index finger drawing a line across her bottom lip. She couldn't help it; she shivered. A full-body shudder that started at the base of her spine and tingled its way up. She hated that he had such an effect on her. It made it impossible to keep her desire for him in check.

She looked up, deep into his eyes. Silence hung between them, and in that moment, they communicated more than any conversation they'd ever had.

Desire, plain as day, danced in his eyes. She knew it by the way his chest heaved, the way his eyes zeroed in on her breasts... And she'd bet her entire savings if she pressed her palm to his chest, his heartbeat would be going a mile a minute.

But there was no chance for her to respond. No chance for her to even register what was about to happen, because it just...happened.

His lips smashed down on hers, and he groaned into her mouth. It vibrated through her body, settling low in her stomach and awakening the parts of her she'd been trying so hard to keep undercover.

He was an expert with his lips and tongue. Their mouths tangled together in a frantic rhythm, and when his hand pressed against her lower back to pull her close, exactly where she had always longed to be, she moaned into his mouth. Every inch of her skin ignited at the direct contact. Her nipples were hard, and there was no hiding it when they rubbed against his chest.

This was how she'd always imagined kissing Cole Murphy would be like. The all-consuming explosion of two bodies desperate for more.

But then he tensed, waking her out of the desire-filled stupor, both of them stepping away from the kiss at the same time.

She sucked in a hard, shaky breath and brought her fingers up to press against her throbbing lips.

He looked like he'd just seen a ghost. As if the sight of her, needy and wanting more from him, was the scariest thing he'd ever seen.

"I'm...sorry. I didn't..." He ran a hand up the back of his neck, and it ended up fisting in his hair.

She stared back into chocolate eyes that were finally showing her something more than icy distance. But when she opened her mouth to speak, nothing came out.

Say something, damn it. Words!

When she didn't say anything, his expression softened into a frown. "Let's just forget we did that."

She had been like a cat in heat, unable to maintain any kind of coherent thought. Maybe that was what happened when you repressed three years of sexual tension.

He wanted to forget it. He'd been the one to pull away,

rejecting her just as quickly as he'd kissed her. Unfortunately, she didn't think she could forget the kiss so easily.

Her shoulders slumped forward and her chin dropped. Her body was still primed, buzzing with need for him, but Cole was right to pull away. She couldn't bring herself to make her fantasy a reality. She had too much to lose. She couldn't risk another career move being subject to an affair.

"I'll wait for you out there." He pointed to the living area and walked out.

Being horny every minute of the day was not the drama she'd anticipated having to deal with when she'd stepped on the plane for Hawaii.

She was going to have to get her head in the game and off of Cole's body, if she had any hope of winning that cup.

. . .

With nervousness in his stomach, Cole sat with the entire Foster clan at the resort steakhouse. All thirteen of them, including baby Hannah.

"So, Cole. Tell us about yourself." Harold sat at the head of the table, his arm around the chair of his wife who sat beside him.

"Dad, really, don't you read the papers?" Cathy said as she battled with Penn to take the seat beside him.

Penn let out a heavy sigh and relented, allowing Cathy to lower into the seat to his left. Penn had no choice but to walk around the table and sit beside Ian.

He wasn't sure if the separation was a relief or a nightmare. That kiss…

Had been a huge mistake. Now that he knew how

explosive it was between them, how could he ever go back to just being friends? Every time he looked at her, like right now, he wanted to lower his zipper and sit her down on his cock.

"I read quality publications, dear." The sound of Harold's voice was enough to nip his daydream in the bud. "Not gossip rags."

So noted. Penn's father didn't approve of the Madewood notoriety. Cole was going to have to wow him with other skills.

What? *Wow?* Since when did he have to wow anyone? He was here as a friend, not a *boy*friend. He was here to help Penn win that stupid cup. Nothing more.

Then don't kiss her, asshole.

"Well, sir. I'm a chef. I have my own restaurant in Toronto. I was adopted by a wonderful woman, and I have three adopted brothers."

"And you're Pennelope's boss," he said.

Cole couldn't figure out his tone. It was half disdain, half curiosity. But he wasn't going to let it faze him.

"Not really. It's the Madewood Corporation that employs her. " He might be an owner, but Neil was the businessman, overseeing the day-to-day operations of the corporation. Cole just wanted to cook.

He looked over at Penn, who bit down on her bottom lip and picked at her fingernail on her lap. Who the fuck *was* this woman? He didn't know if it was her family or the awkwardness between them because of that kiss that had caused her to retreat into herself. Her insecurity twisted in his gut. For the first time since she'd sat across the table, he wanted to reach out and comfort her.

"But Penn always seems to do what she pleases." He looked over at her and winked. "No matter who's in charge."

Dave scoffed. "Pennie disobey orders? Highly unlikely."

The rest of the table smiled in agreement. Suddenly, her quiet, introverted act all made sense. She was hiding from them. These people had a certain image of her, and she was too afraid to rock the boat. He'd bet she believed her real personality would elicit outright disapproval.

That vibrant light in her eyes, the light he hated and loved equally, dimmed whenever they were around her family. But family was supposed to love you no matter what. It made him angry that they wouldn't immediately embrace the amazing woman she'd become. And that just wouldn't do.

"We've been to all three of your family's restaurants," Ian said from the other end of the table. "All top notch. Delicious food."

"Thank you."

"Cole makes the best chicken lime tacos I've ever eaten," Penn blurted, doing her best to pretend she didn't care that Dave was holding his finger near her face, but not touching. Apparently, Dave hadn't grown up.

But once again, Penn had come to his rescue to further validate his cooking skills, because that's what she always did, had always done, for three damn years.

Why had he kissed her in the bathroom? All it did was scramble his brain and make him forget why he was really here. To return her kindness and help her win that cup. At least he'd had enough sense to walk away before he fucked her.

Don't be a perv, Murphy.

"Tacos?" Cathy laughed. "Well, he definitely learned the way to your heart."

"We had to have them once a week when we were kids because of Pennie," Dave explained.

"Well, I'd make them every day if she asked." It's not like he could ever verbalize a thank you. Cooking was the only way he knew how to say it, without having to say it.

"Sounds like something a boyfriend would say." Christine smiled at him from across the table. She seemed like the quiet one, but so far, the blatant teasing had come from her.

He was not boyfriend material.

"You two have separate rooms, right?" Cathy looked horrified. "Because Mom and Dad didn't let Ian and I sleep in the same room until we were married."

Penn groaned, and not in pleasure. She hid her face in her hands, mumbling her words. "We're not dating, Cathy, of course we have separate rooms." Then she looked up, right at her father, as if the validation of their "just friends" status was necessary.

"You Madewood boys sure do love the spotlight," her mother said, then quickly took a sip of her pink-colored drink. Her blond hair was sculpted into a perfect bob, which she habitually tucked behind her ears.

Cole's stomach dropped. He hated when the conversation turned to their celebrity status—a side effect of being adopted by a rich socialite. But it was something he wanted no part of. "Some of us more than others."

"I thought it was just awful how someone put your brother's private moment online last year," Cathy said.

Last summer, Neil and his girlfriend, Carson Kelly, were taped having sex in the kitchen of his new restaurant, before they had opened the doors. Luckily, the business hadn't suffered because of it.

"I called Pennie as soon as I saw it," Cathy said as little Andy snuggled up between them and sat in her lap. "Some people have no boundaries."

"Cathy might have a Google alert set for 'Madewood,'" Ian said, outing his wife.

She waved him off. "You make it seem like I'm a stalker."

"Not a stalker, honey." Ian winked at her from across the table. "Just nosy."

Cole hated the fact that people wanted to be nosy and get the details on his private life. He did his best not to indulge in anything that might be considered a good news story. If there was going to be any press on him, he wanted it to be about the Boys and Girls Club, not about who he might or might not be screwing.

The interrogation continued while they ate their meal. Mostly from her siblings. Penn's father remained quiet at the head of the table.

Cole scarfed down a T-bone steak with scalloped potatoes and a Caesar salad. It was delicious. His steak was cooked to a perfect medium-rare.

When their plates were cleared, Penn visited with her niece and nephew at the other end of the table. She was good with them. Smiling and happy. Interested in what they had to say. She'd be a great mom.

Parenting was something Cole had never learned. It wasn't until Vivian had taken him in that he'd experienced the unconditional love of a real parent. But after the many years as an alone and neglected child, what if he came by those traits honestly? If so, he should steer clear of procreation.

"Perfect timing," her father said as a server brought around a tray of champagne cocktails.

Without a second thought, Cole asked the server, "Can you please bring one glass of straight champagne?" Penn was a purist at heart, at least with her alcohol.

The server nodded, delivered the rest of his drinks, and then rushed off.

"The time has come." Harold clinked his glass while Margot rustled under the table.

Cathy was ready to sit beside her husband, so she switched seats with Penn, who sat down beside him with a smile. Her sweet lilac scent infused his senses. It was better than the scent of any gourmet meal he'd ever eaten.

"This is what we're playing for, children." Her mother placed the infamous Foster cup on the table. The entire family, with the exception of Penn and himself, gave a collective sigh.

The trophy was exactly as Cole had expected. Something that you'd find in a high school athletics case. The base was dark wood. Two sides were covered with gold plates that identified the winners.

Poor Penn. She'd spent the last twenty years striving for something that was completely out of her reach. A matter of pride for the woman who, on a daily basis, expertly battled the media and developed marketing blitz campaigns. But sports? Not so much.

Determination washed over him. He wasn't leaving this island until her name was on that trophy. He owed her this. For all the moody, broody grunts she'd had to put up with over the past three years, it was the least he could do.

"I am officially ringing in the 2015 Foster Family Fun-cation," Mr. Foster announced.

The children cheered from their seats. Andy slapped his fork against the table, and Sara danced in her seat to her own music.

Cole couldn't wait for Finn and Veronica's baby to arrive so their family get-togethers had one of these adorable kids to fawn over.

Harold pointed down to the trophy. "Beth and Dave, you are the returning champions."

"Five years in a row," Beth boasted, looking over at Penn and staring her down.

Okay, someone was a little too competitive.

Penn fidgeted beside Cole. The need to protect blazed inside his chest, coupled with a sense of ownership. He wanted desperately to wrap his arms around her shoulders and pull her close, but that would only make things more complicated.

"Cole, this trophy is now twenty years old." Her father held it up. "Because of the special occasion, I have arranged for a very tough, very meticulous scavenger hunt as the final event."

"Yes!" Dave yelled out. "We kill at scavenger hunts." He held up his hand, and Beth high-fived her husband.

Penn leaned in and whispered, "The key to the scavenger hunt is splitting up the list. It's been my biggest disadvantage." She smiled a devious grin, apparently forgetting about the humiliating kiss they'd just shared.

But she was right to. The scavenger hunt was why he was here. Awkward kisses be damned.

"Not this year," he said. "Not with me here."

She tilted her head, and it was just about to rest on his shoulder when the server came up beside her. She straightened. "Oh, do you think you could—"

He placed the flute of plain champagne beside her.

"Thank…you." She smiled up at the server, then looked over at Cole, and her smile grew even wider. "Thank you."

He shrugged. It wasn't as if she hadn't made it clear on more than one occasion that champagne was not to be trifled with.

When dinner was over, the group walked out of the restaurant and congregated in the hotel lobby.

"Cole," Ian yelled over an impromptu serenade by Sara. "We're going to walk on the beach with the kids. Do you and Penn want to join us?"

"We'd lo—"

Penn squeezed his arm tight. "I need to get the hell out of here," she whispered in his ear. "Drink?"

Cole glanced between Ian and Penn. He knew where his loyalty lay. With Penn. "Maybe tomorrow night. I'm a little tired from the flight this morning."

"Sure. I get it." Ian waggled his eyebrows and gathered up the children's sweaters and toys.

They were just going for drinks, Cole reminded himself. Man, did Ian have it all wrong.

Chapter Four

Penn hiccupped. Too much champagne. If she could have slapped her face without looking like an idiot, she would have. This whole scenario was just asking for trouble.

For once, she had been looking forward to the Foster Family Fun-cation because it meant a break from temptation. But here it was, temptation with a capital *T* in the living, breathing, all-too-tempting flesh.

She'd touched that flesh. Practically humped that flesh back in her bathroom. Her insides heated just thinking about that kiss, but she tamped it down.

Don't go there. He stepped away from you, remember?

Cole returned to the bar, tucking his cell phone in the pocket of his cargo shorts. He'd left her alone for a few minutes to let his brothers know he'd arrived safe.

"How are your brothers?" she asked, spinning the champagne flute between her fingers.

"Good." He settled into the seat beside her. "Keeping

busy. Lots to do even without launching the club."

"Right." She tried to act casual. This was the first segue she'd had since she'd found out the spot on the board was vacant. And this was exactly where her head should be, in business, not analyzing a heated moment that they both knew was a mistake.

"You'll have to fill the board seat now that Gloria has decided to step down."

He nodded, then sipped his beer, refusing to look her in the eye.

"Any ideas who you might get to replace her?" She downed the rest of her drink in hopes her face didn't give away her interest, or her poor attempt at fishing for information.

"We haven't formally discussed anything yet." His phone buzzed in his pocket, but he didn't bother looking. Instead, he smiled. "Finn wanted me to tell you that you're in charge of showing me a good time."

I'll show you a good time, cowboy.

No, no she would not. Funny how she'd changed gears from career plans to sex in one-point-five seconds. She seemed to be good at that since she'd let him maul her mouth only a few hours ago in the middle of talking about his family.

But his words solved the mystery she'd been struggling with since he'd shown up at the pool.

"They sent you here, didn't they?" She cocked her head, waiting for an answer.

He'd been running himself ragged trying to get the club up and running. She knew an impromptu vacation wasn't his idea.

When he nodded, she smiled. "Nothing's going to happen while you're gone," she said.

"I know."

She remembered the day he pitched the idea for the Madewood Boys and Girls Club to his brothers. He'd shown up at Bistro just as she was leaving. But she couldn't very well leave while he was so flustered. And it had broken her heart. She'd seen the pain in his eyes. Seen the tears he refused to cry. And she'd spent all night in his office, just sitting silently with him. She knew the kid being stabbed to death weighed heavy on his shoulders. For some reason, he blamed himself.

She'd decided right then and there that she'd do whatever she could to back his idea. Because she knew that if she ever needed him, he'd do the same for her.

Case in point—spending an entire week with her crazy family just so she could try and get her name on a dumb trophy.

He sat facing forward, his feet on the lower rung of the high stool, his legs wide open, taking up way too much space for her liking. He always crowded the area around her. Even when he was twenty feet away.

The bartender, an attractive man in his twenties with piercing blue eyes and golden skin, wiped the wood bar in front of them, cleaning up the condensation from their drinks.

She pushed out a breath. Damn, he wasn't the only one who needed to relax. Let loose. She'd felt stifled all day. Unlike her usual self. He'd wanted to take a walk on the beach with her family, but she'd made him choose. She'd had enough of the Foster clan for one day. She wanted some me-time. As a bonus, she was also getting some Cole-time in the process.

"Let's do something." Now that she was separated from her family, she felt like herself again, and the anticipation of trying something new danced in her stomach.

"I'm a little tired from the flight." He slumped in his seat, that so-sad face taking up residence once again.

"You would think growing up with Jack Vaughn, you'd know how to have fun."

From what she'd heard, and read on the internet, Jack had been the wild Madewood brother. The love-em-and-leave-em type who had women all over the world and VIP status at every party. Present-day Jack was happily married to her best friend, Sterling Andrews.

He sat back in his chair, his body still facing forward, but his head swiveled to look at her. He leveled her with an unamused sneer. "I don't think you're in any position to be judging, *Pennie*."

She returned his sneer with one of her own. "Ha ha."

"Did you maybe forget to tell your family that you're the life of the party?"

"My family is...complicated." Okay. It wasn't really that complicated. She didn't want to disappoint her parents. Having a daughter who bucked at every rule and ideal they had wouldn't garner parental pride. So she kept a low profile. Although, until Cole had brought it up, she hadn't realized just how different she became when she was around them.

"Bullshit. You're afraid to show them who you are."

He swiveled in his chair, and his leg brushed against hers. The coarse hair rubbed against her skin and sent a shiver down her spine. Body hair wasn't supposed to be sexy or an aphrodisiac. But with Cole, everything about him had her engines revved.

"I am *not* afraid."

She'd never admit that he was right. But she *was* afraid. Of her brothers' criticism. Of not living up to the woman her parents expected her to be. But most of all, of not earning her father's love and respect.

And you would wash all that down the drain if you pursued Cole.

"I just… It was rough trying to live up to my father's standards. Not to mention anytime one of us did anything wrong we had to drop and give him ten."

Which was why she had arms of steel. Silver lining.

"Wow. Maybe *you're* the one who needs to loosen up." He laughed. And it warmed her heart. She loved to see him laugh and smile. It didn't happen very often.

There was a reason he was so guarded, so fearful of getting close to someone. And she knew it stemmed from his childhood—both his mother, and later, the foster care system.

Maybe if she got a little alcohol in him, he'd finally open up. Explain why he was so sad all the time. Why he was so opposed to letting her—or anyone—in. Above all, even her libido, she wanted his trust.

She called over to the bartender. "Four shots of tequila, please."

The bartender nodded and turned to grab a bottle from the back of the bar.

Cole leaned in, his fresh scent washing over her, causing her thoughts to hiccup. "Are you trying to get me drunk, Ms. Foster?"

The bartender placed the shot glasses on the bar and filled them to the top.

She handed Cole one of the shots. "To the Foster Family Fun-cation." She held up her shot glass. "And to finally winning that fucking cup."

Cole nodded and clinked his glass with hers. She lost sight of him when she tilted her head back and let the fiery liquid coat her throat. They both reached for the second shot.

This time, Cole said their toast. "To building a club that will make a difference." He reached out and held his glass up to hers. Of course his toast would have something to do with saving people. He let out a heavy breath, and some of his sad expression dissipated with it. "But first, to finally having some fucking fun."

She smiled and clinked her glass to his. "Here, here." She sucked in a deep breath. The second shot went down worse than the first. "And I'm just the right crazy person to take on that challenge."

He shook his head with a laugh. "You definitely make me crazy."

What kind of crazy, Cole?

"My first suggestion… You need to take that stick out of your butt and loosen up."

"Is that right?" He swayed in closer. His knee brushed the inside of her thigh, and the contact sent a shockwave through her system.

Something was up. Cole Murphy never got this close. Ever.

If she looked up into the sky, would she see pigs flying?

"You can have fun anywhere, Penn. I hate that about you, but admire it at the same time."

A compliment. Sort of. Definitely weird. She laughed. If she didn't know any better, she would have thought Cole

Murphy was flirting with her. And doing a pretty damn good job, considering the man was all business and no play.

Penn laughed to herself. Sweet, sweet Cole. If he wanted to play with the big girls, he'd best put on his big boy pants.

The closer he leaned in, the more her insides heated. The alcohol was working its magic on him. They were making progress— He was actually talking. Steering away from their usual relationship, built on supportive silence.

Because right now, the kind of fun she wanted to have involved him in her bed. Naked. Thrusting. And whispering dirty things in her ear.

Her core spasmed the more detailed her thoughts became. Screw professionalism. Even if she did have a chance at the spot on the board, she knew Cole would never let sex cloud his decision to hire her.

That kiss had ignited the very fire she'd known would exist between them if they gave it the opportunity. Maybe they could play by the "what happens in Hawaii, stays in Hawaii" rules. If no one knew about their encounter, then her career moves could never be questioned.

Besides, right now she was feeling the need to break out of the stereotypes her family had placed on her, and a fling with the object of three years' worth of her fantasies was the exact way to challenge that.

Game on.

"You're right. I do like to have fun." She ran her finger down the back of his hand where it rested on his thigh. "And there's a specific type of fun I'm thinking of right now."

His eyes lifted quickly and wordlessly locked on hers.

She gave him her best dirty-girl smile. "I know all the reasons why we shouldn't, but I can't stop thinking about that kiss." Her finger moved up and traced his forearm, then circled in the crook of his elbow. "Maybe we should explore whatever *this* is." She ran her finger back and forth between them.

He swallowed hard, then gulped in a breath. "Why here? Why now?"

"Can you think of a better place?" She held out her arms, coaxing him to take in the luscious scenery, feel the gentle breeze, smell the fresh ocean air. "I know you want to." She didn't think it would take much to turn him on, but convincing him to actually go along with it, well that was the bigger task. "No one has to know. Ever."

She reached out and grabbed his hand, then settled his palm against her thigh. It twitched. And that simple reaction told her everything she needed to know. But she wasn't ready to stop playing. Even if he pretended he didn't, he loved it when she teased him. And he deserved every bit of it. "I've often wondered what these would feel like between my legs."

Fire blazed in his eyes. "I was afraid you'd be a talker."

Did he not like the dirty talk? She sure did.

Moving his hand higher, she pressed his fingertips against her center. He tried to pull away, but she held his hand in place and locked her thighs together. When he stifled a groan, she knew she'd won.

"I knew the moment I saw these hands that you'd know how to handle a woman." And so he had no question as to where she was going with this, she added, "How to handle every inch of *me*."

With her other hand, she traced up and down his fingers resting on the bar. He made no attempt to move his hand from between her legs. And that muscle in his jaw was twitching like crazy.

"This isn't a funny game, Penn." His voice was thick, heavy with desire, and he demonstrated by rubbing the edge of his finger against her panties.

"This…" She shivered. "Is no game." She meant every word she'd said. "I want to have fun here, too. And sex just happens to be my favorite way to have fun."

He'd probably thought that by coming to this island he'd help her win a cup, but he had no idea he was also going to help her find release from her familial chains.

He blew out a long breath. The more blatant and aggressive her words, the more fear darkened his gaze. "Why are you so willing to offer yourself to me like this?"

Because I've only dreamed of fucking you for three entire years. It's about damn time.

"Maybe this is my way of repaying you for helping me finally win."

He tensed up. "That's not the reason."

"I know." She brushed her hand through his hair, soothing his tension. "And it's not why I'm offering myself to you. You know why." She sat back and locked eyes with him. "You've always known."

At least she hoped he knew. Because there was no mistaking their sexual tension. It was as heavy and thick as the smoke from a five-alarm fire.

He hadn't said no yet. That was a good sign. If he was going to turn her down, he would have already done it.

"Isn't there something you've always wanted to do? Something you've fantasized about?"

He cleared his throat and brought his stool closer to hers. But he wasn't trying to get closer to her, he was trying to stop her from talking so loud. She knew by the way his eyes kept darting to the bartender and the few other guests who sat at tables only a few feet away from them.

"Nothing?" she coaxed. "A little role play, maybe. Sex tape?"

He shook his head vigorously.

Point taken. His family didn't have the best track record with sex tapes.

His legs were scissored with hers. She wondered if he realized his finger continued to caress her center. But if she just scooted forward, she could lock his knee between her legs. Rub out the ache, prove that she wanted this badly. But he just stared at her blankly. He was too controlled to voice his needs.

"What about handcuffs?"

"Christ, Penn. Would you lower your voice?" He looked around her to where the bartender stood, but he was oblivious.

"No one's listening." She bent forward and whispered, "Besides, the fact that you have your hand between my legs tells them everything they need to know." She opened her legs a little more, giving him greater access to the scorching heat that now radiated all over her body.

A rumble sounded from his chest as he graduated from a gentle caress to grabbing the crotch of her panties, the backs of his fingers pressing against her slit. He made a fist and jerked her forward by the sturdy lace.

She lightly licked his earlobe and whispered, "What if I told you I want you to take me back to my room and fuck me?"

He gulped. "You...*like* talking like that?"

"You mean talking dirty?" She hadn't moved away from his ear, but he didn't have to answer. "Mmm-hmm. It turns me on."

His breath was warm against her neck. She was slowly breaking down his resolve. He was getting closer to her, his back moving farther from the chair with every word she whispered into his ear. But she wasn't there yet.

"What turns you on, Cole?" She flicked out her tongue again and licked his ear. "Would it turn you on if I said you'd be the first to conquer my tight little ass?"

His back hit his chair in a sharp movement, but he was smiling. The tiny vein that throbbed in his neck, and the way he squirmed in his seat, confirmed his desire for her. He was going to say yes. He just needed a little more coaxing.

She placed her hand on his thigh and traveled north until her fingers touched his pelvis. Looking up into the chocolate depths of his eyes, eyes almost black—as black as the cloud of sadness he carried around with him—she wished she could change that. To soften him somehow.

She squeezed her thighs, trapping the hand that still gripped her panties between her legs.

Through a heavy breath, he whispered, "You're a tease."

Dating a coworker was never a good idea. But sex wasn't exactly dating. One time in the sack couldn't ruin her chances for being appointed to the board, could it?

Besides, she needed to feel like herself. Being with Cole brought out the best in her. And her family was nowhere to be found, nowhere to question her motives.

With a tilt of her head and long, languid swipe of her tongue across her bottom lip, she whispered, "I'm not exactly teasing, am I?"

Chapter Five

Cole knew if he said yes, it would be a mistake. A big, risky, potentially-monumental-disaster mistake.

But that didn't stop him from sliding his fingers against her slit. It didn't stop him from pushing his knuckle between her folds. She shivered when he groaned, reveling in the wetness that greeted him.

"I'm going to kiss you." The words came out on a choked breath. He didn't have any dirty words or actions. But he knew what he wanted.

Penn.

She leaned forward, close enough that her lips grazed his ear. "Then what are you waiting for?"

They had tried this before, and it had been a disaster. His nerves and his conscience told him it was wrong.

But there was nothing wrong about this.

How could there be when his entire body was aching, throbbing, to bring every fantasy he'd ever had about Penn to life? And that was a lot of damn fantasies.

She was right. No one would know but the two of them. And when the vacation was over, they'd go back to their regularly scheduled bickering.

Do you really believe that?

With one last, lingering look, a look he hoped revealed all the pent-up sexual tension and attraction he'd been harboring for the last three years, he kissed her.

Her mouth worked with his in perfect unison, and the instant his lips had touched hers, all his tension, all that underlying tightness of anger and guilt, seemed to melt away, leaving them only in this moment.

A moment that had his mind racing and his heart beating triple-time.

"Take me to my room," she whispered.

His hand slid down her head over her midnight hair. He sucked on her neck and moved up to whisper into her ear. "Lead the way."

She tensed for a moment in his arms, then softened, her breath heavy against his lips. "This doesn't change anything…at work?"

He was an adult. He could separate lust and business.

He shook his head. "This doesn't leave the island."

He'd made it his mission to keep out of the spotlight. The more focus on him, the more opportunity for people to pry into his past, exposing his demons to the world. And those demons needed to remain buried under the twenty feet of concrete he'd put in place twenty years ago.

He was hyper-aware of her beside him on the walk back to her room. The air practically crackled between them, and when he placed his hand at the small of her back, when he guided her out of the elevator, he was sure he saw sparks.

While she looked for the key in her purse, he checked that no one else was in the hallway, then swiped her hair away from her neck and pressed a kiss to her shoulder. The door beeped, and he held his hand out before pushing them into the quiet space. As soon as the soft click of the door sounded behind them, she twirled in his arms, and he pressed her into the wall, stealing a kiss. She deepened it, snaking her leg up and wrapping it around his hip. When she began to circle beneath him, he wrapped an arm around her back and pulled her up, slamming her breasts into his chest.

He reached down, placing his hand on the backs of her thighs, and lifted. She fit perfectly into his body, wrapping her legs around him as he walked them to the bedroom and placed her gently on the bed.

Her blatant proposition at the bar and her explicit sexuality had been overwhelming. It brought up memories of his past. Memories he never wanted to associate with Penn.

But here he was, a slave to his cock, taking her up on her offer. When they kissed, his demons no longer plagued him, which was why he was here, despite knowing the potential for public scrutiny, despite knowing he would ultimately do something stupid to fuck it all up—her job, their friendship. His whole damn life. Because he had an overwhelming feeling this was going to change everything.

He plundered her mouth with his. The soft whimpers she let escape between their torrid kisses shot straight to his groin.

He pulled away and looked down, taking in every luscious inch of her. He'd never noticed the flawlessness of her skin until he'd kissed it. The softness of her hair until

he'd touched it. The ruby red color of her lips until he'd con-
quered them.

He settled beside her, pulling her leg over his, letting
her warm center nestle against his thigh. Her head fell back,
and he suckled sweetly against her throat, moving down the
corded tendons to her collarbone. Then he kissed the swells
of her breasts that peeked out over the edge of her dress. He
pulled down the fabric. He wasn't one for wasting time.

She hadn't worn a bra, and when he released the zipper at the back of the dress and slid it from her body, he
exposed her tattoo. Brown, white, and pink marked her skin.
A cherry blossom tree spanned her entire side from hipbone
to under her armpit. She wore the tiniest panties that only
accentuated her body—tight and curvy. *Perfect.*

He kneaded her breasts, her nipples stiffening under
his touch. His mouth followed, biting her supple flesh. She
moaned and her back arched, pushing her breasts farther
into him.

"Cole?" she moaned.

He'd always loved hearing his name from her lips. But
now, like this, the way she'd said it in that needy tone, was
like a drug. And he was a desperate junkie.

Her hand clasped his cheek, and she turned his face to
look at her. Her eyes were wide, thoroughly roused from her
slumber.

She was in. All in.

They held their gazes for a moment, and the silent ex-
change between them was as loud as a freight train. One that
could very well ruin everything between them.

But with the way his cock throbbed, and the feel of her
body vibrating beside him, there was no going back.

And fuck, he didn't want to.

This is temporary. This stays on the island.

He brought a finger up to trace her lips. She opened her mouth and slipped his finger inside, sucking with long pulls. Her plump lips were sexy as hell.

Shit. If she could do that with a finger, just imagine—

She let it go with a loud *pop*.

He dipped down and latched on to one nipple while his hand traveled down and traced her pelvic bone.

"Tell me," she moaned out the words. "Tell me what you want." She arched into his mouth.

He stopped and looked at her, opened his mouth, but nothing came out.

"Shy?" She sat up, pushing him off her body, and ran her hands up his chest. "You know there's nothing you can say that will scare me away. Whether it's out there in the daylight, or in here, in bed, when you're ramming your cock deep inside me."

He wouldn't bet on it. She did not want to know what was going on in his head. Sexual or otherwise. Inside his head was one big mess of emotions. And she wasn't ready to deal with the mess he'd lay on her. Probably wasn't even capable of it.

"Nothing you want to say?" she asked softly.

Fuck, yes. There were a lot of things he wanted to say. Had wanted to say for the last three years. But every single word would have led them to the same place—Penn bent over, her skirt gathered around her waist, shaking that perfect ass, teasing him to enter her from behind.

"Don't tell me you haven't thought about this. About what you'd do to me in bed." She kissed his neck. "What I'd do to you."

If she only knew.

He shook his head and pulled away. *Christ.* Couldn't they just have sex? Hot, amazing, *wordless* sex?

She was always talking. Always wanted to talk. He just wanted to fuck.

"I…" He swallowed hard. "Yes. I want to have sex with you."

She shivered in his arms. "Just plain sex. Nothing kinky…?" She bit his earlobe, then licked a line up his ear. "Nothing a little dirty?"

He tensed, memories of his childhood flashing through his brain. The faceless voices of the men who'd grunted and moaned their instructions. He'd heard it all through the thin walls of his bedroom. Eventually, he'd stooped to stealing — had taken a CD Walkman from a discount store — just to drown out the sounds of his mother and those men.

"I just… I've never liked talking like that."

She scooted backward on the mattress and settled her back against the headboard. Her chest rose and fell with long, deep breaths. "Let me show you how much *I* like it," she murmured.

With one finger crooked under the silky fabric of her panties, she pulled them aside and exposed her perfect, creamy mound. She was shaved everywhere but a small patch above her folds. Perfectly trimmed. *Perfectly Penn.*

She gestured with her chin, giving him the go-ahead to take this party further. He reached out with one finger and gently traced the line of her sex. Up and down, feather-light touches that had her hands fisting the sheets beside her.

Her head fell back against the pillow. "More," she

moaned.

He slipped a finger inside. Immediately she opened her thighs wider for him, giving him the room he needed to slip past her folds, to find her wet heat.

He sucked in a breath. She did like it. By the feel of the warm, wet flesh under his finger, she *loved* it.

Her body tightened as he swiped his thumb over her clit. He circled her sweet spot, loving the way she undulated and writhed beneath his touch.

Penn was a strong, independent woman who took what she wanted and never caved to others' demands. She was perfectly capable of knowing what she wanted in a sexual partner, of knowing her boundaries. Maybe voicing his desires wasn't the horrific thing he'd made it out to be.

An overwhelming need to taste her washed over him. He wanted to know the exact spot he needed to suck to drive her wild. He swooped down and licked her folds. She hissed when his tongue made contact, and pressed into his face, rubbing herself against his mouth.

He clamped on to her hips and held her in place. She wasn't going to control this. He might not be able to say it, but he wanted her to scream in pleasure. And it wasn't going to be from her grinding on his face. No, he was going to lick her to orgasm. Fast. Hard. Intense. And she was going to be a puddle in his hands when he was done.

He continued his advance on her, storming her warm center with strong licks and gentle sucking. She moaned. And when he looked up, her eyelids fluttered in ecstasy. It was the same sound and the same face she'd gotten every time he'd made her lime tacos.

Shit. He'd never be able to make those again. Not

without fucking her first.

He gripped her calves and pushed her thighs toward her chest. Spreading her legs, he held her open. He dipped down and kissed her left thigh. Then her right. With each touch of his lips she shivered. He kissed the top of her sex, then her folds, lightly, teasing, making her want it so badly she was begging.

But he knew, deep down, she wouldn't be the only one begging tonight. Because that's what Penn did. She got him so dialed up that he didn't know which end was up.

And that's when he realized he didn't care that he lost control when he was with her, because maybe Penn was exactly the safe space he needed to release some of his own demons.

He stopped his teasing, settling in, licking long lines up her folds, then on her clit. He sucked it into his mouth, and her hips shot off the mattress. She bucked against him, but he maintained his position. He kept it up, drawing out shivers and moans.

"Fuck, fuck, *fuck*…" she whispered as her head fell back against the headboard. Her foot stomped on the bed beside his face. "You're so good…"

He suctioned his mouth over her sex as his tongue worked double-time on her clit.

"That's it," she panted. "That's it. Just like—"

He pressed a finger to her core and massaged her entrance.

"Oh, God. I'm coming."

She broke apart. Her legs clamped against his ears, but he didn't let up. He tongued her until her muscles relaxed. The lighter her body became, the lighter his licks. He swirled and swiped his tongue up and down, from side to side, gently caressing her pink, swollen flesh.

Moments later, she grabbed him by the hair and pulled his face from her body. "Break," she whispered.

Her head was still resting back against the pillow. He crawled up her body, planting feather-light kisses against her stomach, each nipple, the hollow of her neck. He hovered over her, aligning his face with hers. She raised her hand and brushed her thumb across his lips. A timid smile appeared. Then she kissed him. Fierce. Appreciative. Wanting more.

They broke apart, and she panted against his mouth, "I want to know everything about you, Cole. Let me in." She placed her hand against his heart. Her palm was hot, moist from their lovemaking.

She pressed her lips to his again, but this time, it was the most intimate gesture he'd ever experienced.

He felt like he needed to say something, but he couldn't. Not now. Maybe not ever. Not when he knew every word he said would be catalogued. Analyzed. And that was too dangerous. Because he knew, without a doubt, that every word he spoke would be the truth. And there would be no taking it back.

Instead, he returned his hand to her and rubbed her clit with his thumb. The moment her red-stained lips sought his, she lifted up and pushed his fingers inside her body, moving his hand just the way she wanted, fucking herself with his fingers. Taking from him exactly what she needed.

But once again, she wasn't in control.

He took over, thrusting into her center and holding her hips down on the mattress with his free hand.

He made long movements, dipping inside her, then pulling out to circle her clit. Pushing inside, then pulling out.

Over and over and over again.

"Yes, yes—"

Her breath was heavy on his neck where she'd buried her face.

"Yes, yes...*ye*—"

He yanked his hand away.

"Fucking hell!" Her eyes burned, drilling into him. "I was—" She panted. Unable to catch her breath. "*So* damn close. Why did you—?"

"I need more."

He slipped his hands under the waist of her panties and pulled. He kissed his way down her legs as he dragged the satin toward her ankles, then kissed the tops of her feet after throwing the tiny scrap of fabric to the floor.

He rose to his knees, whipped off his shirt, and let his shorts fall to the bed. He grabbed her around the stomach and pulled her up onto all fours. He positioned himself behind her and grabbed his cock, then stroked it up and down her folds. Teasing her.

She looked over her shoulder, her eyes desperate, needy. "I have condoms in my suitcase."

Christ. He wasn't even thinking about condoms. He was too desperate to get inside her.

He nodded, scrambling out of the tangle of his shorts, then followed the gesture of her chin to the corner of the bedroom. He rummaged in the top compartment and found the box.

He sheathed himself in mere seconds, then returned to her perfect bottom, kneeling between her legs. He pressed the tip of his cock insider her, then pulled out. Over and over, reveling in the sounds of her moans.

Then she got greedy. Before he had the chance to pull out, she rammed her bottom backward, and he was balls deep into the most impressive woman he'd ever met.

He grabbed her ass cheeks, squeezing them tight, knowing if he continued, her ass would be pink from his manhandling. Something inside his chest swelled at the thought of leaving his mark on her.

He used his arms to bring their bodies together, his hands grasping the flesh of her bottom. It was so perfect. So creamy. And she was loving it all. Everything he had to give.

He was mesmerized by the sight of his cock disappearing into her. The louder her moans, the faster he thrust, the harder he smacked his hips into her ass.

It was all too much.

He came with a roar. Much too quickly. Emptying every last drop of his pleasure inside her.

They fell in a tumble of limbs onto the bed, and he pulled her against him, hot and sweat-soaked.

Sex for the first time with someone was never this intense for him. This all-consuming. But he and Penn had known each other for too long, and they'd let the attraction between them crackle until it caught fire.

Now that it had, he needed to stay strong, focused. Because as soon as they left this island, that attraction would have to be extinguished.

Chapter Six

Penn awoke to a gentle breeze wafting through the sliding glass doors. The view from her room was spectacular. The sun glistened off the ocean, palm trees swayed in the wind, and the gentle sounds of exotic birds reminded her that she wasn't at home.

And so did the warm arm draped over her torso. It wasn't often that she woke up with a man in her bed. Not because she'd never had men in her bed, but because she'd preferred they hit the road once the bell sounded, signaling the end of their intimate match.

But she wasn't kicking Cole Murphy out of her bed. No way, no how. Not fucking likely.

She lay there, taking it all in—the sounds of nature, the soft cadence of his breathing, the heat of his body pressed against hers. If someone had told her two days ago that Cole would be in her bed, she'd have laughed—silently lamenting the depressing reality, but laughing nonetheless.

She slipped from under the sheet and dropped her feet to the cool hardwood floor. She stretched her back, bringing her arms up and clasping her hands together high in the air with a deep breath. She glanced over her shoulder at the man sleeping soundly.

The sheet had conveniently been pulled from his body, leaving his chest and abs on full display, his man-parts barely covered. Seeing him here in the bright light of day, in her bed, confirmed that last night had, in fact, happened. It was not a dream.

And wow. Even her dreams had never been so amazing, so vivid, or mind-blowing. She'd finally given in to her lust... And it had been even better than she'd ever imagined.

She slipped on a floral silk robe that hung mid-thigh and tiptoed to the bathroom, then quietly made her way to the main area of the small bungalow. A white couch sat on the far wall of the living area in between two matching wing-back chairs and a small table. Another sliding glass door led out to a small patio with an amazing view of the ocean. Which is where she would be sitting as soon as she got some caffeine in her veins.

Outside the front door, a tray with coffee and juice had been left outside the room, just as she'd asked. She placed the tray in the small kitchenette, then poured herself a cup.

Immediately the strong aroma woke her from her haze. But it wasn't an alcohol haze. It was a sex haze. Cole Murphy definitely knew how to get a girl drunk on sex, on his kisses and touches.

She took her coffee to the patio and settled into one of the chairs. She breathed in deep. The air was so fresh, so intoxicating, compared to back home. Like she could start her day with a clean slate every morning, regardless of how bad, obnoxious, or horny she'd been the day before, thanks to Cole's arrival.

The ocean waves mesmerized her. Surfers crashed over the white ripples, and she longed to be athletic enough, brave enough, to go out on the water and paddle herself to exhilaration.

A few minutes later, the bedroom door flew open, and Cole stood in the doorway. Damn, she could get used to that sight every morning.

He rubbed at one eye with the heel of his hand. His dark hair stood up at all sides. He'd thrown on his shorts, but his chest was gloriously bare, the sprinkling of dark hair the perfect amount to run her fingers through and set her mouth to watering. She knew just how coarse that hair was. How it felt rubbing against the soft skin of her back. Against her nipples. She suppressed her shiver.

He yawned with a loud exhale and finally noticed her on the balcony. "Do we have any coffee?"

Once again, her gaze strayed from his face. Who would blame her when she had inch after inch of bare skin to ogle? But when it dipped below his abdomen, her eyes widened. Staring back at her was his morning stiffy. She hadn't remembered it being so...substantial. She hadn't gotten the opportunity to touch it last night.

She took a sip of her coffee, sneaking a peek over the rim. Although she wasn't really sneaking anything. She blatantly admired, tapping her finger on the edge of the ceramic, unable to shake the grin from turning up the sides of her lips.

"Really, Penn?" Cole's disgruntled voice forced her eyes

up. He stood in the doorway, running his hand across the back of his neck, unable to look her in the eye. "It's biology. Can't help it. It's not that I want to jump your bones."

And why not? He certainly had last night, and it had been fantastic.

"I know all about morning erections. I've seen my fair share," she said casually.

He grunted. "Coffee?"

"Over there." She motioned to the trolley.

Shit, he was distracting. On his way over, she crossed her legs and squeezed them together. She couldn't help it. Just the sight of him had always made her horny, and after last night, now that she knew just how good it was between them, she didn't think she could ever get enough of the man.

His bicep flexed when he picked up the carafe. His abs rippled with every small movement of his torso, just screaming to be licked.

On his way out to the balcony, he grabbed his phone and joined her in the warm sunshine. "You stare at my body any harder and your eyes are going to bug out of your head."

"What can I say…" She zeroed in on his shorts. "That jackhammer is hard to ignore."

He settled into the seat beside her, bringing with him his musky scent, making her want to set down her cup and run her hands all over him, pressing her nose against his skin. Or maybe lick his body. Yes. Definitely lick.

Before he took a sip of coffee, he whispered, "So you're saying you like what you see."

"You know I do." She reached out, letting her index finger slide over the soft skin of his shoulder, down his bicep to his forearm, settling on the hand that held his phone.

She wondered if anyone would notice if they didn't surface until Thursday's scavenger hunt. She'd much rather keep Cole hostage in her room than suffer her siblings.

Instead of watching her finger, his eyes bore into the spot where her robe had ridden up her leg, exposing the side of her ass. She had learned last night, and from the marks on her bottom this morning, that Cole Murphy was very much an ass man.

A soft breeze washed over her skin, tightening her nipples. The hard points strained against the softness of the silk draped across her body. A quick look to his shorts proved she wasn't the only one aching.

She reached across and palmed his semi-erection. "I think I'm not the only one who likes what they see." He sucked in a hard breath when she squeezed her hand, his cock stiffening in her palm. "Tell me."

He smelled of sex, and man, and everything that made her head spin. And now, with him right next to her... Her stomach flip-flopped with anticipation. Sometimes it was the lead-in, the verbal foreplay that got her engines revving. A simple phrase. A string of words. And she was a goner. But Cole's silence eased the excitement in her stomach. She had to admit, his aversion to dirty talk was peculiar. But sometimes actions spoke louder than words.

"You could show me." She grabbed his hand and placed it on his erection. "Pull that bad boy out and stroke it for me."

He stiffened. The lustful way he'd been looking at her had suddenly vanished when his eyes glazed over and discomfort washed over his face.

Just when she thought she'd made progress with him, he

took two steps back.

"Is everything—?"

A loud knock sounded on their door.

Once again, he was saved from having to open up.

With a defeated sigh, she stood and headed to the door. Lifting on her toes, she looked through the peephole and cursed under her breath.

It was Cathy. Damn her family. Could she not have one minute of peace to admire the hot half-naked man in her—?

Shit!

She turned to where Cole paced the balcony, and her mouth practically fell to the floor at the sight of him. Those shorts were riding so low on his hips, one tiny tug with her finger and they'd probably drop to the floor.

Nervousness and shame tightened in her stomach, and she raced over to grab his bicep. She couldn't help the small whimper that escaped when her hand clamped around his warm, hard flesh.

Focus, Penn.

"You need to hide."

"What?" He looked at her like she'd gone off the deep end. Maybe she had. At this moment she felt like she was drowning. Like every decision she'd ever made to get her career on track was now rendered null and void by him just being in her room.

"Cathy's at the door," she spat.

The last thing she needed was for her family to create some conspiracy theory about her relationship with Cole. Even worse, what if she did get the offer to be on the board? Would her family think it was because she was screwing him?

She looked around him to the railing. Maybe he could jump off the balcony? But when she couldn't see the ground, she knew it was too far a drop.

"Are you seriously contemplating me jumping off the balcony?" He laughed, but it was a nervous laugh.

She looked up, pleading, "Please. Hide."

His shoulders dropped and he gave in, letting her pull him toward the bedroom. She pushed him over the threshold, and he tumbled inside just as another loud knock sounded on the door.

Cathy's voice penetrated the room. "Pennie, are you in there?"

"Stay here," she whispered. Pointing to the door with her thumb, she said, "I'll get rid of her."

She gently shut him inside, then walked with super-speed toward Cathy, righting her robe and tightening the tie around her waist.

When she opened the door, Cathy barreled in. "Good morning, sleepy head."

Even after four cups of coffee Penn was never that perky.

She watched as her sister-in-law toured her hotel room, peeking into the kitchenette and the balcony. She even glanced into the open doorway of the bathroom.

It was obvious she was looking for Cole.

"What's up, Cath?"

With a defeated look, Cathy stopped her inspection. "You didn't answer my text." Her blond hair was pulled up into another high ponytail. The clip holding it together matched her pale blue fingernails.

"I'm barely awake." Penn crossed one arm over her chest and rested her hand in the crease of her elbow.

"We have lots on the itinerary today, including breakfast and volleyball…"

Penn tuned out.

Yay. More family time. Exactly how she wanted to spend her time when she had a half-naked Cole hiding in her bedroom.

"Dad made us reservations tonight for—"

Fuck me.

Penn zeroed in on Cole's coffee mug sitting on the small table on the balcony. This whole situation was overwhelming, so much so, that she was being careless.

"Pennie"—Cathy tapped her foot on the floor, bringing her attention back to the conversation at hand—"are you coming with us?"

Right. Volleyball. Dinner. Family time.

But when Penn didn't answer right away, the smile on Cathy's face disappeared, and her shoulders slumped forward. "I thought you'd want to spend time with the family since we never see you, and—"

"I'll be there."

Penn silently scolded herself. Cathy was genuinely excited for the family to be together. Even though excitement wasn't the first thing that came to mind when thinking about the Foster clan, this was a good opportunity to spend time with her niece and nephew that she barely saw.

Cathy did one more not-so-subtle perusal of her room. "Will Cole be joining us?"

Penn wanted to say yes. But she didn't have any expectations where Cole was concerned. He was here to help her win the cup, which meant she only needed him for the scavenger hunt. Although last night they'd agreed to explore a new facet of their relationship. One she was hoping she could explore once more before she had to leave for breakfast.

Wrapping her arm around Cathy's shoulders, Penn guided her toward the door. "I'll meet you downstairs in the lobby."

With one foot out the door, Cathy turned, inhaling a deep breath as if she was going to speak.

But Penn beat her to it. "Good-bye, Cathy."

With a heavy sigh, she closed the door and rested her forehead against the wood. She was going to have to be more careful about the time she spent alone with Cole. She couldn't risk her family seeing them together. She couldn't risk having to justify that her potential promotion had been earned on her own merits, and not because she was sleeping with Cole.

She jumped when his voice sounded behind her. "There's an itinerary?"

When she turned to face him, amusement sparkled in his eyes.

"Harold Foster leaves nothing to chance." She pushed off the door and made her way to the living area. "He likes when we're all forced to spend as much time together as possible."

When she reached him, his gaze lowered to the floor. "I'm sure you want to spend time with your family. I'll stay out of your hair until the scavenger hunt."

She didn't want to push her luck. For as much as she wanted Cole as a buffer between her and her family, she wasn't going to force him into mandatory family time. But she'd be lying if she said she didn't want him there. For all of it. Every dinner. Every activity. Every dumb conversation.

"You mean playing volleyball with my family isn't number one on your to-do list?"

She'd never admit this to his face, but she needed him this week. She didn't relish having to face the wolves alone.

"Well…" He threaded his hand through his beautiful brown hair. He was standing only a breath away now. Somehow they'd gotten closer to each other, close enough that she could see his erratic heartbeat pulse in his neck. "I don't have anything better to do."

Suddenly, the air around them changed. The fear, the nervousness that had overwhelmed her moments ago, had vanished and was replaced with lust. That sinful feeling that poked at her libido every time she was with Cole. Especially now, with the way his eyes, like heated lasers, burned up every inch of her body.

"You started something that afternoon in the bathroom when you kissed me." He swallowed hard.

"I kissed *you*?" She laughed. Cackled was more like it. "You kissed *me*."

It didn't matter who kissed first. *He'd* solidified it last night when he let her put his hand between her legs in the bar.

She poked her finger into his hard chest. His pec rippled under her touch. *Fuck, that was hot.* If she pressed into another spot, would he do it again? She forced herself to focus. "You look at me like I'm the only item on your breakfast menu and you haven't eaten in weeks."

"Such a selective memory."

"I remember *perfectly*." She gulped down a breath. "You loomed over me. Talking about soft hands and touching my mouth."

He reached out, his finger doing exactly what he'd done yesterday, sliding across her bottom lip. He leaned in and whispered in her ear, "Like this?"

She swallowed hard, then nodded as a soft, "Yes," escaped her lips. "And then you—"

He attacked her mouth. His lips moved over hers in perfect synchronization. Warm, wet tongues clashed against each other. The sex last night had been hot. But this kiss, this kiss was scorching.

Her heart thundered. This kiss laid all their cards on the table. Because it was acknowledging that they both wanted this. That they were both ready to drop the gloves and go ten rounds in the bedroom. And then win that trophy.

She snaked her hands up his chest at the same time his hands traveled down and slid under the fabric of her robe to cup her bare ass. His skin was warm and firm. She loved the sensation of her palms scraping over rough chest hair. She kissed him harder as she wrapped her arms around his neck, pressing into him, practically climbing on top of him because she couldn't get enough. Didn't ever want to get enough.

He pulled away, and both of them were panting. Then he dipped his head and bit the top of her shoulder. A shiver slithered down her spine, blossoming heat between her thighs.

"Tell me what you're thinking," she whispered in his ear.

Without even a touch to her good parts, Cole was able to get her hot, ready, and wanting to spread her legs. He was her kryptonite. But she feared it was only one-sided.

"Tell me you want this as much as I do."

After last night, she knew she needed to find a cure for her Cole-lust. Otherwise, a week from now, she'd be in big trouble. Giving in to her desire while in a tropical paradise was one thing, but giving in at home was an entirely different, and unprofessional, story. There was no way she was sacrificing the best job she'd ever had—and risk the label of sleeping her way on the board—for a good lay. A great lay.

He straightened out their bodies, and his hands moved from her ass to her waist, then cupped her breasts.

"Please, Cole," she whispered. "I need—" Her chest heaved when his hand lowered and fiddled with the tie of her robe.

When she looked up at him, he hesitated. That same hesitation she'd seen the night before, and only minutes earlier when he'd shied away from touching himself, flashed across his face.

He opened his mouth, then closed it, wanting desperately to say something, but he just couldn't.

This time-out was doing nothing to reduce her desire. The heat from his body was still singeing her skin. Still tightening and curling up her insides so she felt she had no other option but to burst from the seams.

She clasped her palm on his cheek and lifted his head to look deep into his eyes. He could say anything he wanted, and it would rev her up. He could say "T-shirt" and she'd be a puddle at his feet.

He gave her a half smile. "I want to have sex. With you."

Relief washed over her as she kissed his lips, running her fingers through his hair. "I like that thought."

When her hand paused near his mouth, he quickly turned his head and sucked one of her fingers into it. Heat bloomed between her legs, and she let her head fall back on a gasp.

The man may not be able to tell her in the manner she craved, but he knew exactly what *she* wanted. Exactly what she needed.

Him.

He sucked lightly on her finger, then let it go. He bent to nuzzle her neck and tongued her skin with open mouth kisses.

Her core ached. She wanted this man inside her. Inside every part of her. With more want than she'd ever experienced. The fact that he was trying to give her what she wanted... Well, didn't that just tug on her heartstrings and make her want him even more.

More than was appropriate. More than she'd ever get from him in return.

She shook off the blistering need. This man wasn't *the* man. He was too closed off and judgmental. He may not even be capable of love. She saw it in his eyes and everything he did. Distant. Aloof. Solitary. And she needed someone to love her for the woman she really was, the Penn she was every day with him, not the facade she put on when she was with her family.

If she was going to fall in love, she wanted a man who was all in. One who was willing to get naked—body and soul. One who accepted her just as she was. No reservations. No games.

But just for the here and now... Who could resist such an incredible man?

His hand slipped between her legs, and he cupped her sex. He groaned when he found bare skin and swiped his fingers between her folds. She knew she was wet. Just the sight of him in the doorway this morning had her warm and achy.

But now, with his lips on her skin and his hands in the place she needed them the most, she was positively ready. Ready to beg. Ready to give in to anything he wanted.

No, she didn't want to fall in love with Cole Murphy. But fuck him? Oh, yes. She'd wanted to do that since the day she'd walked into Bistro for her very first interview.

She shivered again as he circled her clit. Her pleasure increased with each soft swipe of his finger and when he slipped two inside her, she groaned and shook in his arms. Fuck, who was she kidding? She didn't need dirty talk. She didn't need to play some coy little game. His thumb continued its assault on her clit while he slowly, surely, brought her closer and closer to reaching the pinnacle.

She had no idea sex with Cole would be so explosive.

She needed to soak it up. Savor it. Revel in it. Get in as many dirty minutes with him as she could, because as soon as they set foot in Toronto, they would go back to being just friends, and the walls he'd built up between them, the same walls that disappeared a little every time they were intimate, would once again leave her in the dark.

Which was exactly why she couldn't give this man any more than her body.

She walked them over to one of the chairs in front of the sliding glass doors. A gentle breeze blew into the room, cooling her down from the heat of his kisses. He whipped her around to face outside and wasted no time tearing off her robe.

He placed his hand on her lower back and guided her to bend down. She braced her palms on the seat of the chair. She looked over her shoulder and spread her legs, letting him know she was ready. Willing. Wanting exactly what he was pulling out of his shorts.

The water crashed in front of them. Palm trees swayed and birds chirped. The surroundings were romantic. Beautiful. It was the complete opposite soundtrack for the out-of-this-world sex going on in the room.

Cole grabbed on to her hair with one hand and the other grasped her bottom. He squeezed hard, and with the strength of his grip, he was also opening her up, exposing the one spot she'd never given up. But she knew if Cole suddenly switched gears, she'd be on board.

"Condom," he grunted.

She felt the loss of him immediately when cool air settled over her bare bottom. But he was back to her in no time, the condom wrapper already open and falling to the floor before he reached her.

When he was sheathed, he thrust inside her, hard and fast. Sweat broke out across her skin as pleasure built higher and higher with every one of his strokes. He pulled her hair and her head snapped up. She lifted one foot and placed it on the seat cushions. The change in angle was exactly what she needed to tip over the edge. A few more thrusts and she was soaring, tumbling into the vortex of an orgasm that tightened her entire body.

She grabbed the cushion for balance when her inner muscles shuddered.

He grunted behind her. "Fuck, fuck, *fuck*." Two quick pumps and he bellowed, his pelvis flush against her ass as he convulsed inside her.

Long moments later, when they had both steadied themselves and their breaths weren't as heavy and staggered, he pulled out and stepped away.

She was suddenly cold, empty, and it reminded her how much she felt this way every day. Void of a real connection. A connection that was more than just about sex.

She had that connection with Cole. Even before they'd had sex, they were connected, whether they'd wanted to admit it or not. They had…something. And it was exactly that something that got her out of bed each morning. The thing that kept her satisfied, even though she was alone. Because she knew, if she really needed to, she could call him, and he'd be there. Even if it was only to open a jar of pickles.

Which made it even more important for this thing between them to be kept a secret. The less people knew, the easier it would be for them to slip back into their normal roles when they returned home.

Eventually, the only proof she'd have of their fling was her memories. So she was going to spend the rest of their time making them as memorable as possible.

• • •

As he watched Penn bend to pick up her robe and slip it over her shoulders, Cole felt alive. More carefree and light. Maybe even stood a little taller, straighter. All because he'd just fucked the woman of his dreams. And he'd fucked her real good.

In his thirty-two years on this planet he'd never felt so good about himself. Never had he thought having sex with Penn would be the elixir to his life-long bad mood.

However, last night and again this morning, she'd pushed him much too close to the boundaries he'd welded into place a long time ago. Penn had a dirty mouth… And he liked it.

Which was a hell of a surprise. With her, it was somehow intimate. Trusting.

She'd dipped into frightening territory, bringing back a flood of memories from his childhood he'd kept hidden, suppressed. But she was opening his eyes to a new world, to a new way of looking at his past, which somehow made it less damaging.

"We should get to breakfast," she said as she brushed past him, but he grabbed her arm and twirled her around.

He might not be able to give her what she wanted in bed, but he could definitely give her his athleticism.

"I want to be there for everything on that itinerary." He pressed his body against hers. His cock, still hanging out of his shorts, pressed against her stomach. "It's a good way to scope out the competition so we can win that trophy."

That was a good save. A great save. She'd be surprised to find out he wanted to spend time with her and her family. But no one was more surprised than him.

It made him feel like shit. Vivian had given him the very best family imaginable, and he was grateful each and every day for her generosity and love. Spending time with the Fosters felt like cheating. But this… This was a chance to pretend he was the star of his own after-school special. To erase his own childhood.

She crossed her arms over her chest. "I honestly didn't think you'd care."

She was giving him the challenge face. That sexy I-dare-you look that never failed to get his cock erect. At home, he didn't have the luxury of doing anything about that face — of testing just how far she'd be willing to take it. But here, he had every opportunity to challenge her right back. They just needed to make sure there was no one around to witness their exploits. The last thing he needed was a tabloid scandal.

"I do care." He swiped his finger down her chest and pulled aside the robe, exposing her cleavage. He couldn't deny it. He missed it—her cleavage. Her wholesome family attire left too much to his imagination.

"I miss these. You're not dressing nearly naked enough for my liking." He pulled the fabric even farther, exposing one entire breast. She gasped, stumbling back until her legs pressed against the couch.

She cocked her head and rolled her eyes. "My family doesn't want to see my cleavage."

"But I do." He leaned in and sniffed her neck. God, he loved her scent. Clean, flowery, but not overpowering.

She shook her head. Her tongue peeked out and wiped across the swollen, most beautiful lips he'd ever seen. "They don't know about my tattoo."

"So you're hiding it." His mind flashed back to the night before, and to the night of Sterling's bachelorette party when he'd seen the boudoir photos of a semi-nude Penn.

She shook her head again, refusing to look him in the eye.

"Why do you let them put you in a box? Here, you're almost nothing like you are at home." It made no sense at all. She was perfect. Successful. Beautiful, inside and out. How could she not want her family to see every part of that?

Finally, she met his gaze, determination washing over her face. "I have no idea what you're talking about."

"Yes, you do." He smiled. Satisfaction at being right coursed through him. But he wasn't going to push.

"Look, you don't know anything about my family—

And they are *my* family." She emphasized the word to get her point across. "So, let's just stick to the plan." She poked him in the chest. "Winning that—"

He cut her off with a kiss. Heat smoldered between them, residual heat from the sex they'd just had, along with new heat. A more potent fire flared—if that was even possible—as their lips tangled with a flurry of moans and whispered curses.

It wasn't hard to see that she liked him calling the shots. Her eyes flared with desire every time he demanded something of her. She had used sex to wiggle her way into his psyche. It had changed him, even if only minutely. So why couldn't he do the same for her?

He rested both hands on her shoulders and pulled away, his breaths heavy and staggered. "I really don't like you," he muttered. At her stifled whimper, he realized his mistake and ran his hands down her arms to grip her wrists. "I mean, I don't like *this* Penn."

He'd surprised himself with that comment. Her inability to filter her thoughts and actions had always made him a little uncomfortable. But seeing her like this...*stifled*, with that vivacious light missing from her eyes, it was hell to see.

She turned away. "It is what it is."

Not if he had anything to say about it.

It wasn't lost on him that every time they were alone together that light returned. Even now, her eyes sparkled with more than just desire. They sparkled with safety. Comfort. While that pleased him to no end, it also made him sad. She had nothing to be ashamed of. Nothing that required approval. Nothing that was the least bit worth hiding. He was going to prove to her that her family would welcome the changes, embrace the real Penn.

When they were both showered and dressed, they headed to the lobby to meet her family.

She was wearing a white dress with flowers. And cute little flip-flops that matched the color of her toenails. She'd piled her shiny black hair on top of her head and had secured it with a pink paper flower. But what should have been cute on any other woman was downright sexy on Penn. He wanted to take that flower and use it to get her off. To stroke the soft paper over her clit and watch as she shook in his arms.

They reached the lobby, and suddenly, Dave grabbed Penn around the neck before bringing her in to swipe his hand over the top of her head. "Are you ready to eat some sand today, Pennie?" Dave played the annoying older brother really well. Like, Emmy nomination good.

"My hair, you assho—" She tore herself away from his grip with a sneer.

In what world did Penn ever stop herself from uttering a curse word? There was that goody two-shoes image again. Cole would have to do something about that.

Baby Hannah let out a wail from her stroller, and Beth immediately bent to comfort her. Everyone's attention swiveled toward the baby.

Penn's entire family was waiting for them. Only Harold and Dave wore the Foster Family Fun-cation T-shirts. This time, the color was a teal blue. Did they have a different color for every day of the week?

Where was his T-shirt?

He huffed under his breath. For the first time since he'd arrived, guilt washed over him. He shouldn't be thinking about iron-on T-shirts. He should be thinking about the club and how it would help so many kids and families. But he was here for a good cause. Not just for his sanity, he was here for Penn.

"I hope you brought your A-game, celebrity chef." Dave pointed at him. "Beach volleyball is my specialty."

"Specialty or not, you're going to lose."

When he looked down, Penn stared up at him with appreciation, maybe even a little awe. She had done so much for him over the last three years without even knowing it. Backing her up with her family, helping her beat them was the least he could do. And he would have done it for nothing, even if she hadn't done her damnedest to come on to him. He was a red-blooded male. There was only so much teasing he could take.

Watching and feeling her shudder in his arms was the sexiest, most erotic thing he'd ever experienced, and he wasn't leaving this island until it happened again. Many, many, *many* more times. As many times as her body would allow. Because even if he was tapped out, he had hands, a mouth, and a tongue that he could put to good use.

Chapter Seven

Penn's mouth almost dropped to the ground when she stepped out of their rental car. Several chickens and a rooster ran around in the dirt. One of the chickens came close, even hopped through her legs as it chased after the rest of the birds.

Cole walked around the front of the car to join her. "We're a long way from five stars, aren't we?"

She looked down at her plastic flip-flops and silently thanked the heavens for her decision to wear them this morning. "You could say that again."

After breakfast, they'd gone back to their rooms to change. He'd shown up at her door, urging her to hurry up so they could meet her family for the next challenge. It was all a little too cute. A little too perfect. And a little disappointing…because after the week was over, she might never see that eager face again. He'd probably go right back to carrying the weight of the world on his shoulders.

She walked up to the sign beside the doorway to the tour office. Pictures of men, women, and children in buggies covered in mud stared back at her. "Wait, this is a *mud* buggy tour company. As in, you ride the dune buggy through the mud?" She whirled around. "On *purpose*?"

She looked up at Cole who was now standing beside her and gave him her best puppy dog look. "I don't. Do. Mud."

"I know." A devious grin curved his lips. "This is going to be so great."

She groaned. "You get way too much pleasure in my pain."

"Don't worry. I'll protect you from the big bad mud." He went to kiss the top of her head, but then retreated, surveying her family to see if anyone had noticed his almost sign of affection.

She stepped away, giving them some distance. Giving herself some space to remember her boundaries. The more time they spent together, the harder it got to keep their hands and lips off each other, even if it was only a tiny peck on top of her head.

The jingle of keys caught their attention when her father emerged from the tour office. "Today's challenge is a mud buggy race."

Her entire family hooted and hollered in excitement, even the little ones who were already covered in mud.

Cole was already flying high from their win in beach volleyball that morning, where she'd scored the winning point. Including the kayak race, they were now up by two. She had no doubt he was excited to make it three.

Attendants fitted them with goggles and a helmet, and they were given ragged jumpsuits to put over their clothes and bandanas to cover their faces.

The protective clothing had seen better days, and God only knew how many people had pulled on these coveralls.

She tied her bandana around the lower part of her face, securing it with a double knot at the back of her head. The only parts of her that were exposed to the elements were her nose, a small sliver of her cheeks, and her feet.

"I'm guessing you don't mind if I drive?" Cole asked as he went to the driver's side of the buggy and hopped in.

The death trap...er, the mud buggy, was completely open—no doors, no windows, just a roll bar. Just great. Given her freakishly poor athletic skills, she'd definitely be the one person in her family to fall out.

After hopping into the passenger seat, the attendant buckled her up. *Seatbelts for the win!* The two brown straps were secured over her shoulders and snapped into place between her legs. Her fears of falling out eased.

Cole started the engine as the attendant ran over some last minute details, including where the GPS was hidden under the dash in case they got stuck.

Rain water. Mud. A scratchy bandana tied around her mouth. A veritable picture of sexiness. She'd be damned if she'd pretend she was loving this. Nothing about it was who she was or ever wanted to be. Thankfully, she didn't have to keep up a facade. Not with Cole.

"Ready, scaredy-cat?"

"I am *not* afraid." She held on to the steel bar in front of her. Her words had come out muffled so she moved the bandana away from her mouth. "Why do you always have to be such a jerk? You know I—" She screamed when the buggy kicked forward, and he drove them to the starting line.

"Good luck, Murphy." Her brother, Dave, and Beth rode by. "Penn can't read a map to save her life."

Dave was so wonderful. It took everything she had not to jump out of the buggy and clock him.

Cole turned in his seat and let his arm rest across the back of the buggy. "You know…" He lifted up his bandana and exposed his lips. Damn, they were beautiful. Plump. Soft. So perfect and capable of bringing such pleasure.

"Penn?"

She shook her head. "Huh? What?"

He smiled broadly. "Whatcha thinking about?" Damn him, how did he always know?

She shook her head. "Nothing." She squirmed in her seat. *Shit*. Now she was all hot and bothered. Sex should be the last thing on her mind right now.

As if.

The conditions weren't exactly conducive to a quickie. "What were you going to say?"

"That if you just once tried talking back to your brothers, I guarantee they'd dial down the insults."

Dave was the only one who openly insulted her. Pete never did. Ian… He was more subtle.

"Is this really the conversation we're having right now?" She didn't appreciate the distraction. She needed all her focus on being miserable. "All of a sudden you're the family whisperer?"

Okay. Maybe he was right. Maybe if she returned their insults and innuendo, let them know she could hold her own, maybe then they'd get over themselves. But actions spoke louder than words. At the end of the week when she hoisted the trophy in victory, it would be all the sticking up for herself she needed.

All four buggies were lined up at the mouth of the trail. Her father stood in front of them, ready to start the challenge.

"You ready?" Cole asked.

She looked over at him and nodded. "As ever."

"It's time for us to kick some ass."

Her heart fluttered. Us. It warmed her deep inside that he thought of them as an us.

She slammed down on the thought, locked her feelings away, and concentrated on the trail. She wasn't here to lose her heart. And she definitely wasn't here to win someone else's. The only winning she'd be doing was in a scavenger hunt. She wasn't looking to see her name on a marriage certificate. She only wanted it etched on that trophy.

Her father pointed to each buggy, and they each nodded their readiness. He lifted both arms in the air and hesitated a moment before whipping them down. "Go!"

The race was on.

All three buggies raced forward. Cole battled Dave for the lead on the right side of the trail.

Despite the speed, the dirt, and the white knuckles, the trail was beautiful. Wilderness lined each side of the asphalt path with tall trees and flowering bushes, and she could have sworn she saw a monkey. Did they have monkeys in Hawaii?

In a bold, underhanded move, Cole veered to the left and smashed their buggy into Dave and Beth. Cole took the lead and stepped on it, trying to catch Pete—who had left his pregnant wife behind for safety reasons.

"We have to go to the right." She pointed up ahead where the road split in two. "And then another hard right."

The trail was damn confusing.

"Got it."

Cole cut off Ian and Cathy, careening onto their exit. The new part of the trail was less traveled. Instead of asphalt, it was gravel. It twisted and turned, splashing mud on her goggles and coveralls.

The sun shone through the trees ahead of them, and a breeze swept over her face, cooling the little strip of her cheeks that was exposed.

"Just follow the trail as it is." She lifted her bandana as she spoke, her heart thudding fast in her chest. "We don't have to do anything until it splits again."

He nodded, but kept his eyes on the road. His hands squeezed the steering wheel tight, with power and skill. Her stomach fluttered at the sight. She knew just how much those hands could do, how strong yet gentle they were on her body.

She gripped the map in her lap, focusing on the beautiful scenery instead of his hands. It really was gorgeous out here. If they weren't in a race against time, she'd wish they had a picnic basket and champagne in the back of the buggy.

"This is awesome," he yelled over the roar of the engine.

She pulled down her bandana. The scratchy thing was driving her nuts. "Not really."

"I wouldn't do that," he warned.

"Stop telling me what to do."

Suddenly, he slammed on the breaks, and she jerked forward. A wave of muddy water cascaded up and splashed all over them.

With a scream, she held her hands out, bracing herself against the dirty water. She gripped the metal bar above as he made a sharp turn. He overcorrected, almost tipping them over. Once again, mud splashed up from the ground and covered her.

Wiping at her goggles, she tried to clean away some of the mud. She looked down at her body, then at Cole. She was much more dirty than he was. Not that he'd have cared if he was covered from head to toe.

He hollered with excitement as they picked up speed and zoomed along the trail.

She took another look at the map. They needed to veer left at the next fork. She saw it up ahead, just after a spot of uneven terrain.

"Slow down!" She pointed at the map. "We need to make a sharp left."

Instead, he stepped onto the gas and bellowed a loud warrior cry.

She squealed. "Cole!"

The trail swerved a hard left, and when he turned the wheel, mud splashed up all around them. The buggy wrenched forward. Her ass went airborne. Thankfully, her seatbelt was tight under the arms and held her in securely. Instantly, the buggy came to a rocky halt.

The front right tire had hit a ditch. They were stuck.

"Nice driving, dude."

He looked over as he revved the gas, shifting from reverse to drive, trying his best to rock the buggy out of the gully.

Finally, he gave up, smacking his gloved hands on the steering wheel.

"Take the wheel," he growled.

She pulled down the bandana and let it settle against her

neck. "There is no way I am driving this death trap."

"You have to. Unless you want to push."

She glared at him. "Fine."

He unstrapped his seatbelt, hopped out of the buggy, and came around to her side. He reached between her legs and unsnapped her seatbelt.

"Slide over. I'll push, you reverse."

She balked. "Why don't we just call the attendant?" That's what they had been instructed to do. "I'm sure they have some kind of pickup that can pull us out of the ditch."

"You want to win, don't you?" He waited a beat as she hesitated. "How long do you think it'll take for them to get here?"

Valid point. Plus, she wasn't keen on actually staying put in one place too long in this forest. Who knew what kind of animals and insects lived in here?

She slid over and did as he'd instructed. He pushed with all his might, grunting and groaning as she pressed the gas pedal. But it was hopeless.

"*Fuck.* I think we're officially stuck."

He shook off the mud from his gloves as he came over to her side. In an unexpected gesture, he lifted her goggles to the top of her head, then ripped off his muddy gloves and tossed them to the floor of the buggy. After reaching across her body, he grabbed one of the bottles of water and opened it.

"Put your head back." She did, and he poured water over her face, gently rubbing with his fingers across her cheeks. "You have mud everywhere." The water traveled down her cheeks and wet her coveralls.

He then did the same to his own face.

He leaned closer, ducking his head under the red frame

of the buggy, and grabbed the white towel that was in their supply bag.

This was the Cole Murphy she had come to love so much over the past couple days. The one who had forgotten the sadness and distance that plagued his everyday life. This Cole Murphy was just enjoying the moment.

He reached for the two-way radio, but she stopped him. "I think that can wait a few minutes."

She tilted her head back and captured his lips. He tasted of sweat and sexy man. And she had a craving for just that.

"What about your family?" He looked around at the woods on either side.

"They won't find us."

With a grin, Cole dove in and deepened the kiss, pressing her back against the seat of the buggy with his torso.

"I want to kiss you all over," he panted. "But I can't."

She moaned, totally caught up. "Why not?" She needed his kisses. Needed them more than the very breath she needed to survive.

"Because there is mud everywhere."

She choked out a laugh and let her head fall back against the seat. "Oh, yeah." She filled her lungs, trying to regulate her breathing. She looked up at the sky. Bright blue. Not a cloud to be seen. And then she looked into Cole's glittering eyes. They were dark chocolate. A nice contrast to the light reddish brown of the mud that was all over his neck and collar.

"I want..." His lips grazed hers, a soft caress she knew would get molten hot if they let it.

"Tell me." Her head fell back, her words coming out on a breathy whisper.

Nipping her bottom lip between his teeth, he made a throaty sound. But he was still mute.

"Do you want me on my knees?" She'd yet to taste his cock. The thought sent a shiver down her spine.

Their eyes met, and he nodded.

He had no idea how much it turned her on, the fact that he was trying, albeit unsuccessfully. But it was all the more sexy.

"Do you want me to touch you?" She urged him on with a tilt of her chin. "Taste you?"

He let out a long breath, and then his shoulders rose as he inhaled, as if regrouping.

"And you." He looked down at her. "Touch yourself?" The flush in his face might be from the race or from whatever sexual hesitation he was working through, but since he'd asked, there was no way she'd say no.

Although she didn't respond right away, the seconds that followed his request were anything but silent. Sexual energy buzzed between them, lighting a fire inside her body that had been on a slow simmer since she'd first met him. But now that she'd had a taste, she had no idea how she was going to extinguish it. "I like the sound of that."

His shoulders fell, relief washing over him as he tightened his grip around her hips.

She slid off the buggy seat and guided them to a dry patch of gravel near the tree line. With quick movements, she undid the buttons of his coveralls, then slid them off his shoulders so they pooled around his ankles. She made quick work of her own, leaving herself enough room to spread her thighs and give him his fantasy.

On her knees in front of him, she removed her gloves and

threw them to the dirt. There was nothing gentle about the way he looked at her in that moment, and with one graceful movement, his cock was out. He stroked his erection a few times, then smoothed the tip across her anxious lips. When she stuck out her tongue, he groaned.

There were no lingering caresses, no tender touches. Just the thrust of his cock inside her mouth. With one hand she stroked him, alternating between taking him deep and fisting him. Her other hand found its way inside her coveralls and stroked her clit. She thrust two fingers inside, and when she moaned around his cock, he pushed in as far as she'd take him and stayed there. With wet fingers, she circled her hard bead in a perfect rhythm — the one that took no time to get her off. The one she had perfected over the years when she'd needed a quick and satisfying release — usually thinking of Cole as she did so.

He wasn't the only one fulfilling a fantasy.

Her pleasure built, and so did his grunts.

His hands grabbed her hair, and he guided her mouth down his cock with long steady movements. She did the same to her clit, but in double time. Within seconds she was shaking, her legs fighting to give out, the gravel pinching her knees. She moaned again, and he cursed as he fucked her mouth.

Her panting grew as she tried to breathe around his substantial length and thickness. She couldn't help it; she bit down when the first spasms of her clit vibrated under her fingers.

She jerked forward.

"Shit, *shit*," he moaned.

As the waves of pleasure spread through her body, she

lost all concentration. She embraced her orgasm, let it wash over her like a hot summer wind.

Next thing she knew, he had released his grip on her hair, pulled out, and turned his body. Her hand continued to jerk his cock off to the side, splashes of his pleasure shooting out and hitting the ground.

She collapsed back on her heels, taking the pressure off her knees, and he stumbled back, resting against a tree. They stayed silent for a long moment, catching their breath.

"Wow." It was the only word that did any justice to how she was feeling.

"Yeah," he agreed, and smiled over at her.

They returned their clothes to their rightful places, then made the call to the tour office.

Cole leaned against the buggy on her side, crossing one foot over the other.

She leaned forward and rested her chin on his arm. "*That* was out of this world."

His lips curved up in a smile, and he let his head fall to the side, catching her stare.

The sex had been hot and messy. And so totally irresponsible. But she'd loved every minute of it. Just like she'd loved every other minute of the time they'd spent together since he'd shown up in Hawaii. Even the non-naked time.

Her decision to have a tropical fling with him was getting more complicated by the second. She'd thought getting him out of her system would be enough to get their working relationship back on track.

But what if she just couldn't get enough?

Chapter Eight

Cole opened his eyes to the morning sun and felt completely at peace.

The birds sang. The waves crashed. Families laughed and played on the beach. Even the air around him was lighter, and that heavy cloud of sadness had disappeared.

Mother Nature was working her magic on this island, and somehow, Penn had worked her magic on him.

It was easy to brush off her effect on him at home, but this trip had smeared the lines of their previously black and white relationship. He'd always chalked up his feelings to lust. She was smoking hot, and the fact that she was his co-worker made it easy to believe there was no true connection between them. She was nice because she felt obligated, or she helped because she was paid to do it. But the more time they spent together without their predetermined roles, the harder it was to believe they were *just friends*.

He was now floundering somewhere in the gray, and the

gray was messy. It was dramatic and attention seeking. He'd spent way too long flying under the radar, keeping his secrets hidden, but now, with one vacation and zero willpower, it could all come crashing down.

He needed to focus on the task at hand.

He'd come here to help her win a trophy. Instead, she was helping him work through his shit. He might never work through all of it. His childhood had been rough, and something he'd carry with him forever, but at least now he knew he wasn't completely broken.

He couldn't wait to return home and launch the Boys and Girls Club. He was rested. He was ready. For the first time in his life, he was hopeful for the future.

And that was some scary shit.

They'd slept through breakfast. Even though they probably could have eaten before going to bed—considering it wasn't until the sun peeked out over the horizon that they'd finally drifted off to sleep.

He slipped his arm out from under Penn's body and got out of bed. She sighed and rolled over, snuggling down into the mattress. The white sheet barely covered her naked body. If he stood staring any longer, he'd never be able to sneak out and make his purchase.

They had the day off from the itinerary. And he needed it. A day to regroup. Between the mud buggy race yesterday afternoon and the Marco Polo game last night, they were tied two-two.

He'd lost focus. He blamed it on that spectacular blow job she'd given him yesterday.

She'd sucked his dick in the fucking woods and rubbed herself to orgasm. And *he'd* asked her to do it.

He shook his head. Even this morning, it was unbelievable.

The Penn who'd gotten on her knees in the woods was the Penn he wanted to see every day. The woman who put him at ease, surprised him and annoyed him equally. He'd seen far too little of her on this trip.

He hurried down to the lobby and took the short hallway that lead to the shopping concourse. It was time for her family to embrace the same woman he did. The real Penn. Not some cowed figment of their imagination, but the wild, loud, cursing beauty that he'd fallen for the moment he'd laid eyes on her.

He had something special in mind for her. He wanted nothing more than to see her as she truly was — happy, flirty, vibrant…and exposing a lot of skin. He missed that amazing cleavage.

When he returned to the suite, she was still fast asleep. He placed the gold foil bag on the dresser and slipped into bed beside her. He traced his hand down her arm to her hip. She stirred. Then he slipped his hand between her thighs.

She opened her eyes and sighed. "This isn't a bad way to wake up."

"We have a free day today." He leaned down, inhaling her sweet morning scent. "No challenges. No family dinners."

"*Mmm*, about time." She waggled her eyebrows. "And I know exactly how I want to spend the day." She reached out and tried to pull him down against her, but he resisted.

"By the pool, of course," he said with a grin.

Her bottom lip jutted out. "I can't believe y — "

He slid off the bed, grabbed the bag, and placed it in front of her.

She immediately sat up, bringing her knees to her chin.

"What's that?"

"I bought you something."

She lunged for the bag. "Really?"

"Nuh-uh." He wrapped his hand around hers, preventing her from opening it. "You have to promise me that no matter what's in here, you'll do it for me."

"Now I'm scared." Her eyes widened. "Is it a butt plug? Nipple clamps?"

He let out a hearty laugh. "I assure you it has nothing to do with sex." He leaned in and nuzzled her neck. "Although, I can't be held responsible for my roaming hands."

She peeked inside but still looked confused. "What the devil is in here?" She sifted through the masses of tissue and pulled out the white spandex and cotton garment.

"A bathing suit?" She looked a little disappointed.

"Not just *any* bathing suit." He held it. The wooden toggles that were attached to the strings clanked together. "A bikini. I think it's time you let your family see just how special you are."

He trailed his finger down her rib cage, circling around and around the cherry blossoms tattooed on her skin.

"I don't know…" She bit her bottom lip, looking worried.

"If there's one thing Vivian taught me, it's to own who you are. It doesn't matter where you came from or who your family is. Your past is your past. Let the world know who you are today."

Which was part of the reason she insisted all four of her sons keep their original surnames. As much as they each wanted to be a Madewood, Vivian believed it was more important for them to carry their past forward.

This was the most candid he had ever been about himself

with Penn. Hell, with anyone. His turn for baby steps. But despite his insecurities, there was one thing he knew for sure.

"I live every day by a code, trying my best to make a difference, to remember there are still kids who have the same life that I once did, who need my help. I may not be articulate like Neil, charming like Jack, or as kind as Finn, but I know who I am. Everything I do is for those kids, whether it makes me look bad or not."

He hoped she'd be satisfied with that small glimpse into his past, because he didn't think he'd ever be able to tell her just how bad it really was.

He cleared his throat. "I know you think your family won't approve, but I honestly believe if you give them a chance, they'll surprise you."

That's what family did. Support unconditionally. Vivian had made him believe that again. Surely, this great family could be the same way if Penn just gave them the chance.

"Even Dave?" she asked.

"Even Dave." He cocked his head to the side. "Trust me. Your family will love you no matter how many tattoos you have."

He pulled away the sheet, exposing her perfect, naked body. Seeing the tiny bruises on her hips didn't cause him guilt. She'd liked it. She'd asked for it. It caused his cock to swell at the memory of what he'd done to put them there and his ego to inflate, bringing him pretty damn close to asshole proportions.

"The way you're looking at me right now isn't making me want to get out of bed and show off my new bikini."

He slipped the bikini bottom over her feet and made his way up her legs, taking the opportunity to kiss his way to the center of her body.

"Having you dress me like this isn't helping, either." Her breathing became heavy and her back arched, but then she giggled and contorted when his fingers tickled the backs of her knees.

"You're right." He smacked her ass, but left his hand on her cheek, squeezing the soft flesh. "Taking off your clothes is more fun." With a wink, he left her to finish getting ready.

After making two laps around the three connected hotel pools, they found two empty lounge chairs and kicked back to relax.

It was a perfect day. The sun shone brightly, without a cloud in the sky. A gentle breeze wafted up to the pool from the ocean, which cooled the heat from the sun on their skin. He reached for the sunscreen.

She kicked off her gold flip-flops and hid them under the lounger. "I'm going to the swim-up bar to get us drinks." She threw down her stuff and turned toward the pool.

"You need sunscreen," he blurted.

She shook her head and looked over her shoulder. "Always following the rules."

"Cancer is a serious issue."

Vivian had died of breast cancer. Although it had nothing to do with the sun, cancer was cancer. It was devastating.

Penn looked properly contrite. "You're right." She walked up to him, her lithe body looking absolutely fantastic in a tiny sundress she'd used to hide the bikini.

After grabbing the bottle of sunscreen, she covered her legs first, then her arms. She even covered her chest and neck, all without taking off the sundress.

"Can you do my...?" She gestured to her shoulders and

the small part of her back that wasn't covered.

"Sure." He stepped forward, wanting direct contact with her body, but she moved away.

"PG-13, Murphy." She gave him her back. "This is a family place."

Did he mention he hated PG-13 movies? With Penn, his thoughts always went straight to a XXX rating.

But she was right. Where was his head? In public, they were *just friends*.

He squeezed out a hefty amount of sunscreen to spread across her shoulders and did so an arms-length away from her body. No one would mistake this for anything but a friendly gesture. He knew even the slightest brush of his cock against her ass and he'd be done for.

She helped him out by scooping up her hair and pulling it away from her neck. Christ. Even distance couldn't stop his cock from responding. Her exposed nape tightened the front of his swim trunks. He suppressed the urge to bury his face in the crook of her neck and spend the rest of the afternoon scenting her.

"If you want to have proper coverage, you're going to have to take off that dress," he challenged.

She hesitated, looking from left to right. If she was looking for her family, the coast was clear. He hadn't seen them all morning.

But she shook her head. "Maybe later."

It was disappointing, but he understood. He was still the luckiest man here, because he was the only one who actually knew what was hiding underneath that fabric. That alone was enough to get him through the day.

Penn returned the favor and covered his body with

sunscreen.

Now that they were both properly protected, she bent over and put the sunscreen in her bag, giving him a perfect view of her behind. It was only half covered by the bikini bottoms. The round flesh was tight, and she sported a fierce tan line from that hideous one-piece she'd worn all week.

"Is it bad that the only thing I can think of right now is smacking your ass?"

Cole stiffened. Did he really just say that? Out loud?

Penn had the same reaction because her entire body went still just before she looked over her shoulder, pressing one finger to her lips.

If this was how it was going to be when they got home, he was never going to be able to stop fucking her.

Cole watched as she slowly submerged herself into the water. The shallow end only came up to her belly button, so she kept going, finally diving under. When she emerged, he swore he saw stars and heard music—that slow, sultry movie music they always played when a sexy girl was in the water. He wanted her to turn around, damn it. To see how beautiful her face was when she thought no one was watching.

Of course, he wasn't the only one staring at her. The guy to his left was pretending to read his book, but it had fallen over onto his lap. And the creep to his right, in an unsubtle move, pulled down his sunglasses to get a better look.

It made him hot knowing that every man within poking distance was jealous. That he got to have her. Every day. Any way he wanted.

At least until Saturday.

He lay in his lounger and soaked up the sun. He could get used to this. Not a care in the world. Sure, he loved his job. Loved creating delicious food for people's enjoyment, including his own. But he needed to get out more. Not to work or program functions, but to real life. He needed to get himself a life totally apart from the Madewood food empire and his overwhelming need to save the children in his city from neglect and poverty.

"Get out of your head, Murphy." Penn had waded to the side of the pool and set two drinks on the concrete. "Don't make me drink alone."

As usual, Penn was able to see the signs of his weariness.

But he couldn't help but worry. Although if he was honest, he was pretty damn proud that he was able to push it aside for most of this trip. He could have been a basket case.

Penn got out of the pool and scooched beside him on the edge of the lounger, water dripping from the sundress.

"You worry too much." She picked up a drink and thrust it toward him.

That, he did. But it was something he couldn't help— He'd grown up worrying. Constantly. If he wasn't worried about the safety of his biological mother, he was worried about where he was going to get his next meal, or worried he'd be caught stealing.

And now, he was worried that his feelings for Penn were dipping into dangerous territory, and if he didn't get a handle on them, he'd surely drown.

"We need to have some fun." She smiled. "Teach me something."

Sometimes he had no idea how her thoughts connected. It kept her a constant challenge. And was one of the many things that drew him to her.

He let his anxiety go and went with it.

"Okay." He jabbed the straw into the frozen, fruity drink she'd given him. "What do you want to learn?"

She shrugged. "Anything."

He thought for a moment, and the result shocked him. He shook his head. "All I know how to do is cook." He definitely needed to get a life.

"I don't buy that. I'm sure you can do lots of things. You just don't give yourself time to do them."

Possibly. Hadn't he just been thinking the same thing minutes ago?

"All right." He sat up and planted his feet firmly on the hot pavement, setting aside the drink. "I know something we can do."

He pointed at two boys walking past the pool area with surfboards in tow.

"You know how to surf?" She stared at him in disbelief.

"Not a clue." Which made the prospect even more enticing. "*Point Break* used to be my favorite movie, though, so I think I can handle it."

She giggled. "Right."

When their drinks were finished, they headed to the rental booth on the beach.

He picked out a blue board for himself and a red board for her. When they were all waxed up and their lines were fastened to their ankles, he led them to the shoreline.

"I really don't think it's a good idea to try this without lessons." She looked out to the water. Her hair whipped across her face, but it didn't hide the worry that darkened her gaze.

"Now who's the rule follower?"

"Fine." Her shoulders eased and her body relaxed. "But

when I fall off every time, no laughing. And remember"—she stepped into the water, looking over her shoulder—"I'm doing this for you."

They had a blast.

Out in the waves, Cole laughed and groaned as he popped up onto his board over and over. It took quite a few tries to stand up without dragging his feet in the water and toppling, but eventually he was able to stay on for a few seconds before wiping out. Penn hung off to the side with a big grin, straddling her board, her feet dangling over the sides, just watching him.

He paddled over to her.

"That was pathetic, Murphy."

"Maybe you're not the only un-athletic one." He felt he'd been moderately successful. But he hadn't expected to ride a five foot swell his first time out.

"Gee. You looked pretty graceful to me as you cartwheeled into the waves."

He made a face at her as he paddled closer and lined up his board parallel to hers. But there wasn't a chance in the world of getting mad at her teasing. He was having too much fun.

Her body was smoking hot, wet, and glistening in the sun. The urge to kiss her was overwhelming. And she knew exactly what he was thinking. She leaned closer, scoping out their surroundings to check that no one was watching. But out here, in the middle of the ocean, no one could see who they were.

He couldn't stop himself from leaning over and locking his lips over hers. Their mouths moved in perfect harmony, a sexy back-and-forth movement of sun-heated lips and pliant tongues.

Whenever they kissed, he no longer worried about... anything. His stomach fluttered each time her lips touched his. She did this to him—gave him this amazing feeling. This overwhelming happiness. He honestly didn't know what to do with it. It was so new and unfamiliar.

With a contented sigh, he pulled away. "Your turn to get up on the board."

"Do I really have to?"

"Yep."

She paddled out and he followed, yelling after her, "Relax your body. When I tell you to jump up, try not to let your feet drag. Find your balance and just let the wave take you."

"I don't want to do this," she shouted.

"Yes, you do. You can do it!"

They waited for the right wave. Tiny ripples and mediocre swells passed under them.

"No, really. I can't do this," she protested as they waited. "One time, my family rented a house on the lake, and Pete took me out on one of those paddle boat thingies." Her arms waved all over the place as she spoke, sending rivulets of water cascading down her face and neck. Pearls of water accumulated on her cleavage, and he wished he were close enough to bend down and lick them off her warm skin. "We got stuck in some weeds or vines or something. I don't know..."

She was so fucking adorable. So adorable that just watching her tell the story made his insides flip-flop with happiness. Frustration grabbed hold of him. Why couldn't her vacation be two weeks long? He hadn't expected their time together to go beyond sex, to move past the alarming chemistry that had crackled between them for so long. But it had. And he was going to damn well enjoy it, because he'd miss this feeling when their fling came to an abrupt end.

He closed the distance between them, then cleared his throat and grabbed her shoulders, forcing her to stop talking and look him in the eye.

"Forget about the damn lake house."

She nodded. "Right. Okay."

"It's just you and me, no judgment. Just fun. If you fall, who gives a shit? I already fell about a million times. Did you think I was a loser?"

She laughed and shook her head.

"Exactly. Time for *you* to fall on your face."

The laughter died. "But, Cole, I—"

In the distance, he saw it. A perfect wave for her to try.

"Paddle. Go! Paddle!"

She squealed and began to paddle, looking over her shoulder at him.

He waved his hand toward the beach, and she finally turned her head forward. "Jump up!" he yelled.

Her ass lifted, and then her feet slid down the board, and she rolled off into the waves.

She popped up through the water and rested her arms on her board.

"Again," he yelled.

Again and again, she tried to ride a wave. Every time she fell. But she got right back up. Each time, staying on a little longer. At one point, she took off the sundress and threw it at him. When her bikini shifted and exposed her breasts, he'd have been more than happy to paddle over and put them back in place. With her back turned to the beach, of course.

As if he needed another Penn Foster image in his spank-bank. After the week so far, it was already overloaded.

Finally, she caught the perfect wave. She jumped up and steadied herself, both feet firmly planted on the board, her knees bent, arms out. Her cherry blossoms were more vivid when wet, the pink, brown, and white ink catching his atten-tion. As it always did whenever she was naked.

She rode the wave like a pro. Then she wiped out.

He paddled closer to where she'd gone under, each wave pushing him closer to her.

Pride filled him each time she got back up on that board. Her family had her thinking she wasn't good enough for pretty much anything. And that simply wasn't true.

A few seconds passed, and Penn still hadn't emerged. Another two seconds. Cole's stomach dropped when bubbles of air reached the surface and burst.

She emerged just as he reached her, breathing in huge gulps of air.

"I did it," she choked out. She continued to suck down breaths, but a tiny smile curved her lips.

Christ. She'd scared the shit out of him, but she was laughing hysterically. He couldn't help but laugh along with her, and it eased away that fear.

"Did you see me?" she squealed. In her excitement, she wrapped her arms around him and squeezed. "I totally rode that wave for like two seconds."

He laughed against her neck and returned her tight hug. "I saw. You did it."

She eased away, wiping the water from her eyes. "I

literally feel like I could fight a giant right now." There was no mistaking the pride and exhilaration in her eyes. "Like I could run a hundred miles."

Adrenaline was coursing through her body. She was high on accomplishment. It was a new look on her. She was usually so confident that she downplayed her actions. But after knowing her for so many years, he was thrilled to see another facet to her personality. And it was just another check on the long list of things he admired about her, lusted after.

She'd wanted to try something new today, and they had. But this had been one long day of athletic foreplay that had gone on long enough.

"I know another way you can use up that energy." He lifted one eyebrow in question, hoping his innuendo was heard loud and clear.

It never took Penn long to catch his drift. Her mind was just as much in the gutter as his.

"I wonder what that could be?" She bit her bottom lip, a move that drove him insane. He wanted that lip between his teeth. Gliding over his cock.

He reached out and cupped her cheek, letting his thumb graze over it. "I can show you, but there's just one more challenge you have to complete before I do."

She cocked her head, a grin spreading across her lips.

"Race you to the beach?"

She gasped, and without hesitation, smashed both hands down on the surface of the water. The splash hit him in the eye, and it was the perfect distraction. She was already bolting for the shore.

"Cheater," he yelled after her.

His chest swelled. And so did his cock.

Penn had been the first woman who had touched a part of him other than what was hidden in his pants. He wanted to shake his fist at the sky every time he thought about it. He couldn't see where things could go with Penn.

This fling was just that. But it didn't mean he wasn't going to spend the rest of the week wearing out his dick.

Chapter Nine

Penn didn't think anything could feel as good as Cole's hands on her body. But she'd been wrong. She'd fallen off that surfboard fifty times, at least, and she'd survived. She'd humiliated herself in front of Cole, and he hadn't cared one bit.

The elevator dinged on her hotel room floor, and she peeked out, making sure the coast was clear.

When she looked over her shoulder and smiled, he grabbed her hand and tugged them down the hallway to her room. She struggled to keep up with his stride and hold on to his hand. They were both covered in sand from where they'd both fallen to their knees on the shore.

After she'd gotten there first.

She rummaged in her bag for the key and slipped it into the slot. She stepped over the threshold, turning to face him, and waited.

He took one more look both ways down the hall, and

then he was on her, kicking the door closed behind them.

Within seconds, he was ushering her toward the bathroom where he turned on the shower faucet, testing the water temperature.

When he turned, his eyes took in every inch of her body. "You're all dirty." His words came out on a groan, like he was trying to stifle his need for her.

He stalked toward her and placed his hand on her cheek.

She looked up deep into his eyes. He always had an edge of fear, of hesitation in his eyes when he looked at her. And she was happy for that, because she feared the moment he let down his guard completely, she might never be able to let him go.

"Let me take care of you."

She nodded. Smiled. He turned her to face the mirror above the sink.

Tenderness. Vulnerability.

Two words not in her vocabulary when it came to Cole Murphy. But right now, he was a completely different person than he'd ever been with her before.

He lifted the sundress off her body, which had been a bitch to squeeze back into when it was soaking wet. It fell with a wet thud to the floor. Then he pulled down the bottoms of the bikini and let them settle around her ankles.

He wanted to take care of her. To please her. She could just sit back and let him do it. She'd never allowed a man to do that before. She was always so concerned with earning things on her own that she never asked for help. Never allowed anyone to give her anything, even if it was something she craved, like intimacy.

Next, he reached up to loosen the string at her back. The

bikini top fell away, leaving her breasts partially exposed. His gentle hands moved up her rib cage, his fingers fluttering over her tattoo. He traced up to her shoulders, the sand scratchy under his touch. When he reached her neck, he swept away her hair and loosened the knot at her nape. He didn't push it off. He let the top slide down her body at its own pace.

He looked up and their eyes met in the mirror. "I want to be gentle with you," he whispered.

She gasped when he dipped his head and his nose grazed the skin at her shoulder. Then her neck. Then the spot behind her ear. She was too sandy for his lips to make contact, but she craved the feel of them on her.

"But I don't think I can."

She turned in his arms, running her hands through the wet strands of his hair. "Just make me feel good. However you want."

If he kept this up, she'd never be able to go back to the way things were between them. Which scared the hell out of her. Not going back meant risking a career she'd worked hard to build on her own merit. If the people around her, especially her family, suspected her success was based on favors and not hard-earned expertise, not only would she have failed at earning their respect, but it would limit her authority and effectiveness in her day-to-day work.

She would not have her many accomplishments with the Madewood family tainted with rumors of their affair.

She'd spent the last three years locking away her heart, trying her best to keep it from slipping into the equation of their relationship. But if he kept this up, if he continued to give her everything she'd thought he wasn't capable of, she was going to have a hard time walking away from him.

He guided her to the shower. The hot water had steamed up the glass walls. She rested her hand on his shoulder when she stepped over the sill and under the warm spray. It felt good to rinse away the sand, but so did the warm glow that enveloped her just being near him.

Her head fell back, and she let the spray wash over her. He stepped in beside her, still wearing his board shorts. But she didn't need them gone to know what beauty hid beneath them—the long, thick pleasure that awaited her. All she had to do was reach out and grab it.

But she didn't. He seemed to have another agenda. So, she'd let him carry it out.

His big hands found her hips and grasped them with the strength of a desperate man. They brushed over her skin, over her arms and stomach, her back and shoulders. He bent and wiped away the sand on the backs of her thighs and between her legs. Her breath hitched with every swipe of his hand. But with the first touch to her folds, she tightened, her stomach clenching with desire. Her legs clamped together, preventing his hand from moving on.

She watched him through the droplets of water that had accumulated on her eyelashes. A tiny smile curved his lips. But he didn't give in to her. He pulled his hand out and continued on, ensuring her skin was free of every grain of sand.

He squeezed shampoo into his palm and rubbed his hands together, then lathered her hair, letting the white foam cover her head. He used his fingertips to massage her scalp from her hairline to the nape of her neck. She let out a tiny moan when he pushed his soapy thumbs against either side of her spine.

"*Mmm*. Maybe instead of a chef you should have been a hair stylist."

His voice rumbled in her ear. "I'll keep that in mind if I ever contemplate a career change."

When he was satisfied every strand had been scrubbed, he rinsed it clean, cradling her head under the steady spray.

Next, he reached for the bar of soap but stopped abruptly, changing course to retrieve her bottle of body wash. He examined it.

"You can use the loofah." She pointed to where the pink poof hung on the faucet.

"I was wondering what that thing was for."

She chuckled.

He squirted way too much gel onto the loofah, then took the same care with her body as he had with her hair. Swiping it in all the right places, every crevice, every sweet spot that kept her heart racing and her breath quick.

"I've never had anyone bathe me before," she whispered. "I'm going to be the cleanest girl on the island."

He gently turned her body under the water, rinsing away the soap, then pressed a soft kiss to her abdomen. It rippled under his light touch. She reached out and tugged him to her, but he slid away from her grip and straightened until his body was hovering just a shadow away from touching hers.

He whispered, "I like you dirty." And then he kissed her.

His words zinged right to her pelvis, tightening the walls of her sex. Four simple words that meant more to her than any piece of bling or pound of chocolate. He was getting good at verbalizing his thoughts.

She snaked her hands up his chest and clasped them behind his neck. One of his hands traveled down to her thigh and lifted her leg. The contact with the rough fabric of his shorts scraped against her clit, and she moaned, arching backward, pulling him closer and harder into her as they kissed.

Their lips moved in a heated rhythm. It had only been minutes since their last kiss, but she was struck with the same intensity, the same overwhelming heat, as if it were their very first time kissing.

His hand on her thigh moved to the center of her body and pressed against her core.

She let her head fall back, panting against his face, exposing her throat. He closed his mouth over the sensitive skin, sucking and licking while she whimpered her appreciation.

"*Mmm*, the body wash made your skin smell like coconut," he whispered against her neck. "I should probably taste test other areas."

She moaned again and brought her head up. Anticipation swelled within her.

"Just to make sure you're clean…everywhere."

Gripping the waist of his shorts, she pulled him closer and devoured his lips with an even hungrier kiss. With a need on an entirely different level than they'd experienced so far.

Pulling away, she gathered her thoughts and senses. "Then what are you waiting for?" she murmured.

He moved her hands aside and let his shorts fall to the tile below. His cock pointed toward her, hard and oh so beautiful.

He grabbed her around the hips and pushed her against the shower wall. She perched her bottom on the narrow tiled seat.

At this level she had a perfect view of his cock. It throbbed, pulsed. He needed release. But before she had a chance to touch him, he pushed her reaching hand away and cupped her breasts. He squeezed and rolled her nipples between his thumbs and forefingers.

"Oh!" she cried, the pleasure-pain streaking through her whole body.

His hands moved lower, his calloused fingers seeking the place she most needed him. Ached for him. His thumb grazed over her clit and her body jerked.

He dropped to his knees and pressed his thumbs to the top of her mound, parting her folds to expose the tiny bundle of nerves. His head dipped, and he licked her, a long swipe of his tongue flat against her eager flesh. Then he licked again. And again. And again. Each time, her body burned, throbbed, pulsed with sensation.

Fuck, he was so damn good at this. He'd managed to get her hovering at the peak of release within a minute. And for as much as she wanted to languish in the pleasure he was giving her, she wanted to come more.

She looked down and their eyes met. The sexiest sight in the world—Cole's hot mouth latched on to her, licking her folds without even coming up for air. But then she noticed his arm. It jerked back and forth under her legs.

"Are you jerking off?" she asked, excitement zinging through her like an electric shock.

He halted, glancing up at her.

Why did he stop? It was the most erotic thing she'd ever seen.

"Don't stop. Any of it." Her back arched, but she righted herself, lowering her eyes just as he returned to stroking, slowly.

She'd always considered herself sexually experienced. Always the aggressor. Always taking her pleasure into her own hands. But being with Cole was opening up a brand new world of sexual possibility. Who would have thought she'd almost orgasm just from watching him jerk off?

When their eyes met, he grunted, his lips and teeth circled, relentless against her clit. "You like watching?" he asked, between licks.

Her entire body contracted, tensing to brace herself against his onslaught of pleasure.

"Watching me stroke my cock turns you on?"

"Fu-uck, Cole." She nodded vigorously, letting out a whimper when he fluttered his tongue against her clit. "It's so damn hot."

In a weird way, they were the perfect sexual match. Drawing Cole out of his shyness, helping him find his way in the bedroom, had taught Penn that she enjoyed giving in, submitting, just as much as she'd enjoyed taking control.

All Cole had needed was a little coaxing to come out of his shell. And damn if he wasn't a quick learner.

She pushed back against the tile, spread her legs wider, and fisted her hands over the ledge. Watching him pleasure himself. "*So close…*"

He moaned and mumbled against her sex, "Come for me, Penn. Come in my mouth."

She was mesmerized by the hand that jerked his cock and the two fingers thrusting in and out of her, the tongue circling between her folds. By the beat of the slick water that hit her breasts and stomach. By the almost stifling fog and heat that scorched her skin.

She detonated, her body tightening, quivering, convulsing to the rhythm of his fingers and tongue.

She heard him grunt his release. His mouth tightening against her mound but still licking.

The pounding water against the tile was the only sound heard above their erratic breathing.

Cole was the first to surface, standing and pulling her up against him. His hands smoothed away the wet strands of her hair stuck to her forehead and cheeks. He smiled down at her and pressed his lips to hers in such a gentle gesture that it brought tears to her eyes.

Then he returned to washing off her body. When they were both clean and had dried off, he carried her out, settled her on the bed, then wrapped her up in the sheet.

"Have a little rest first, but then I have plans for us."

She nodded.

He left the room, the lower half of his body wrapped in a white towel. Whoever decided that hotel towels should be universally white was brilliant...and obviously a woman, because the sight of Cole's tanned skin against the fluffy white was sexy as hell.

She'd thought they were friends a few days ago. But now, after he'd given her so many orgasms she'd lost count, she had no idea what they were. And that was the whole problem.

She'd never be able to justify to others, even to herself, why she'd dismissed her principles for a good lay. Besides, even if she did want to see where things could go between them, there was no way in hell Cole would be on board. He was too focused, too intent on atoning for a childhood that was still a complete mystery, to ever take this seriously.

Chapter Ten

Cole's thumb shook as it hovered over the green telephone icon on his cell phone. It had been there for almost five minutes as he'd contemplated calling the one female in this world who could give him the push he needed. Hell, the one *person* in the world.

He hadn't really realized what he'd done in the shower until it was over. He'd jerked himself off.

In front of her.

He knew it was normal, that there was nothing wrong with dirty talk and all those things he'd always hesitated over. But being the son of a prostitute meant baggage. Things he didn't want to deal with, that he'd rather just close the door on. And if he didn't tell Penn about his past, he wouldn't have to deal with it.

But for the first time in his adult life, he didn't want to feel unworthy of a woman like Penn. Didn't want to *be* unworthy.

He was freer with her, and he couldn't help chasing that feeling.

He'd thought he'd gone into this week with his eyes wide open. Foolish. No matter how prepared he was to maintain his distance, maintain some kind of barrier so that they could exist professionally when they returned home, it had been futile.

With a shake of his head and a deep breath, he hit send.

Veronica's familiar voice answered on the second ring. "If it isn't Mr. Hawaii."

He laughed. "Don't be jealous that I'm in a tropical paradise, and you can't get your pregnant belly onto a plane."

Veronica Whitfield was one of his oldest friends, and soon-to-be sister-in-law.

"You're so right," she moaned in defeat. "I'm frickin' huge. Having four chefs in the family isn't helping matters."

Only one more month until the first Madewood baby would arrive, and Veronica had taken the "eating for two" mandate literally. The woman was always starving these days, grazing on anything within reach. It was endearing and definitely a welcome characteristic, since her husband and his brothers loved to please people with their food.

He laughed. "How are you feeling?"

It took her a minute to answer. "I'm feeling all right. A little crampy, but my doctor tells me it's normal Braxton Hicks contractions. Personally, I think it's because I eat too much."

He chuckled with her. "Is Finn taking good care of you? I hope you're not working too hard."

The questions were just flying out of his month. Mostly out of nervousness. Although, being away from home for the last few days, he was sure he'd missed a lot.

"No, no…hey"—she perked up—"how's Hawaii? Is it beautiful? One day I'll make it there."

He started to answer, but she interrupted him. "Wait. What's going on, Cole?" He heard a clang, probably a spoon hitting the side of a bowl. "You never call just to shoot the shit. It's always with a purpose."

She was right. She knew him too well. Which was one of the reasons she had been on the top of his list of people to call. He could have called Finn. But this time, he needed a woman's opinion.

He was feeling things he'd never thought he'd feel. And he was confused as hell. Even thinking about making things with Penn more than a fling was a disaster waiting to happen. And what happened when they went public? Too much attention meant too many people wanting to know more about him. He couldn't risk his past being exposed. He couldn't risk her finding out his first experience with sex had been hearing his mother with her tricks.

These feelings had to remain in Hawaii. It was the only way to keep his past buried.

"You want to tell me something?" Veronica asked. He heard a rumpled thud. Maybe the positioning of a pillow. "Where's Penn?"

"She's lying down."

Recovering from the massive orgasm he'd just given her. He hadn't meant to take their shower to sexy town. He'd started off wanting to take care of her, to pamper her.

True, eating her out wasn't exactly the care he'd planned on giving her. But it had worked out for everyone, hadn't it?

"I think… I think I'm going to tell her."

Penn wanted him to open up. But the thought of spilling his guts, telling her about all the crap from his past, made him nauseous.

Which was why he was now on the phone with Veronica, asking, without asking, if opening up to Penn was the right thing to do.

"Tell her what?" Veronica's voice was so calm, so casual, yet determined to get an answer.

There were less than a handful of people in the world who knew about his past. Veronica was one of them. They'd grown up together. Shared a lot of the same experiences. She'd seen it all—or most of it.

She was usually so perceptive. Another reason he'd called her. He could have cryptic conversations without having to spell everything out, and she always knew exactly what he was saying.

But maybe her pregnancy hormones were messing with her Cole-receptors today. It seemed she needed things spelled out.

But suddenly she gasped, and his hidden meaning must have dawned on her.

"Is *that* why you called me? You want me to say it's all right to tell her about your mom?"

He shrugged. Not that she could see it. "Maybe."

"If you want my opinion... I think she can handle it."

Penn was a strong, determined, independent, and successful woman, capable of many things. But processing her feelings for a man with a past like that might not be something she wanted to do, let alone would be capable of.

He had no home, no true parenting to speak of, no role models until Vivian Madewood, and all the instability and floundering that came along with that kind of life. People ended longer, deeper relationships for much less.

"Don't you think I'm too big a mess?" he asked.

"A mess? No way." Her response came out so fast it made him feel a little better. The fact that she hadn't hesitated meant she truly believed it. "A huge pain in my ass? Definitely." She laughed. "But I still love you."

A short silence passed between them.

"Cole, what is this all about?"

If he couldn't talk to V, how could he possibly talk to Penn? "Um…"

She let out a long sigh. "Look, I'm going to tell you something you're not going to like."

"Terrific." He braced himself on the couch, letting his hand grip the arm so tight his fingers turned white.

"Cole…"

Here it comes. He was moody. Guarded. Too high-profile and too closed down for the risk to be worth it.

"You're wonderful," she said.

He stilled, letting the words wash over him. The unexpected and completely false statement had caught him off-guard.

"Are you listening to me?"

He shrugged again.

"Stop shrugging when I can't see you, Cole Murphy. You know how much that annoys me."

She should have been a teacher. Or, as her younger siblings always said, a prison warden. Her serious tone was enough to get the hair on his neck to stand up. At times, she was downright scary.

He heard stifled groans and heavy breaths. She was

trying to get up. Over the last couple of weeks he'd really noticed a change in her. She waddled instead of walked. She was slower to do…everything. He'd never been witness to a pregnancy up close and personal before. It was some serious shit.

"As much as I love our conversations…"

He laughed. "Sure, you do." Their conversations were almost always one-sided.

"Finn is coming to get me for a doctor's appointment. But can I leave you with one last thought?"

"Sure."

"You only have to ask yourself one question: do you think Penn is worthy of knowing who you really are?"

In the shower, he'd touched himself without a second thought. Without any thoughts at all, except for the way Penn tasted and the way her moans revved up his own desire. That had to mean something. Something far more important than sex itself.

Hell, yes. She's worthy.

He trusted her, and he knew his secret would be locked in the vault. But more important than her being trustworthy was his decision to trust her in the first place. Exposing his past, his deepest, darkest secrets, meant more than just telling her the truth.

He was falling for her.

And that was even scarier than facing his past.

Now all he had to do was hope he didn't end up a splattered mess on the concrete when it was all said and done.

Cole had flashed his money around once again and arranged with the concierge for a candlelight dinner in a thatched hut on the water. Now the evening had even more importance. Tonight he was going to blow her mind. Not only with the scenery and the romantic gesture, but by telling her some of his shit. The shit she'd been wanting to know forever.

He was ready. He could do this. She wouldn't judge.

He sat on the sofa, absentmindedly flipping through the pages of a magazine while he waited for Penn to finish getting ready.

"Hi." Her voice carried softly from the door of the bedroom.

He looked up from the magazine, and immediately his dick tightened at the sight of her. She wore a short, red dress with a thin brown belt wrapped around her waist. There were no shoulder straps, so it hugged her breasts perfectly. She'd put sunglasses on top of her head, but they were barely noticeable between the black waves of her hair. She'd done something with it. Something to make the shiny strands curly…but not. God, he sucked at describing girl stuff.

"Are you going to pick your tongue up off the floor?"

He snapped his gaze up and looked at her face. He hadn't realized he'd been staring at her breasts the whole time.

"Sorry, I—" He took a deep breath and regrouped. "Damn. You look fantastic."

"Fantastic enough for wherever we're going?" Her body fidgeted, and her eyebrows perked up. "Aren't you going to tell me what we're doing?"

"It's a surprise."

He stood and walked over, and put his hand on her hip. She took his gesture even further and pulled him closer.

"You look pretty fantastic, yourself."

He'd dressed in a pair of white linen pants and a purple-checkered button-down shirt.

She nuzzled his neck, inhaling deeply. "But I do prefer how you look with your clothes off."

He growled. They were on the same page when it came to where their clothes looked best. On the floor.

He smacked her ass, partly to shake her out of the smoldering desire that had flared between them as soon as she embraced him, and partly to keep his own mind focused. "You ready?"

She nodded and threaded her arm through his.

He gestured to the door, holding out his hand. "Your romantic evening awaits, my lady."

They walked through the hotel, turning a few heads. Yes, he could definitely get used to having Penn on his arm. If nothing else, for the ego boost. As far as anyone else knew, they were ideal for each other. Deep down, he knew Penn cared about him. She'd displayed that time and again over the last three years. They'd developed a real friendship, and over the last few days, nurtured a sexual chemistry he'd never experienced with anyone else. But that didn't mean she was equipped to handle his baggage for the long haul. It might tear them apart. Which made his growing feelings for her all the more dangerous.

But he had to try.

They walked side-by-side, being sure to keep their distance until they were behind closed doors, and were greeted at a small boardwalk by Jason, the hotel staff member who had arranged the evening.

"Mr. Murphy. Everything has been prepared just as you

asked."

She gasped, and her eyes turned a shade of cobalt as she caught sight of the small hut positioned on a low cliff above the water. "Is that where we're going?"

He nodded, shook hands with Jason, and handed him a fifty.

Cole motioned Penn ahead of him, but he stayed back and whispered to Jason, "Remember, no interruptions until tomorrow morning."

Jason handed him the key. "Of course, sir."

"Cole, this is so beautiful." Penn had stopped to admire the foliage that lined the boardwalk. "Look at these flowers." Her hands brushed across the lush pink blooms. Off to the right was a rock garden. Between two of the biggest rocks sprang a slow trickle of water that fed into a pond below where several koi swam around, their mouths opening and closing as if they were trying to have a conversation.

The thatched hut was sitting on a deck that had been built into a rock cliff a good twenty feet above the water. Waves crashed directly below them. Pretty damn romantic, especially for his first time trying to pull off something like this.

They walked up the small set of carved stairs that led to the hut's door, a set of California shutters which he unlocked and pulled wide, opening up the space to the warm Hawaiian breeze.

It was a lovers' paradise.

"Oh, my," Penn whispered as she went inside.

At the back was an oversized pillow that acted as a mattress, surrounded by several other small pillows and blankets. The shades of yellow, pink, and blue brightened up dark walls that were made up of what looked like bamboo.

In the middle of the room, a table had been set up for two. A silver bucket sat on a rolling cart beside the table, chilling a bottle of champagne, along with a bottle of Jack Daniels.

On the other side of the table was a makeshift kitchen. Jason had set up a small grill, and a second rolling cart was laden with all his ingredients and cooking utensils.

She whirled around. "Are you going to cook for me?" Her jaw was practically on the floor in delighted surprise. And he was ecstatic that he'd been able to put it there.

He'd never seen her like this, with an edge of vulnerability to her excitement. She was always firm and set in her opinions and statements. But not tonight.

Something was different tonight.

"Cole... I don't know what to say."

He stood by the door, admiring the way she reacted to every inch of the hut. "It's beautiful, isn't it?"

She let out a gasp of awe. "Beautiful isn't the word." She traced the edge of the champagne bucket with her finger as she slowly spun in a circle. "And you did this for me?"

When she looked up at him, he nodded. Her eyes were filled with emotion. And tears. Penn, who didn't cry over anything.

She joined him at the door, and he tugged her into an embrace, her back to his front. He wrapped his arms around her waist and breathed deeply. It wasn't the fresh scent of the outdoors that infused him; it was Penn. Her lightness. Her unwavering support and belief in him.

He didn't want to move. Ever. Even if a typhoon blew across the island, he wasn't moving. Because here he was comfortable. And dare he say…happy. Once they stepped off that plane, there was no way of knowing if this feeling would last.

It was time he told his friend the truth. But first, he had dinner to make.

He headed to the table, grabbed the bottle of champagne, and opened it with a *pop*. Bubbles spilled out with a splat onto the floor as he filled two crystal glasses.

He held out a glass to her, then lifted his. "To good friends."

Their glasses clinked.

"Hungry?"

She nodded and licked her lips. "Starving."

The first thing he did was fire up the grill to get it nice and hot. Next, he made citrus marinade for the mahi-mahi. He squeezed the juice of an orange and lime, then combined it with oil, salt, cilantro, and some honey.

While she was delighted with the champagne, she must have noticed he hadn't taken more than a few sips of his. "Ready for something stronger?" she asked.

"That'd be great."

She mixed him a Jack and Coke and placed it near the grill for him. It was amazing that she always knew exactly what he liked, what he needed.

She shifted in her seat, searching for something on the ingredients cart.

"What, no dessert?" She batted her eyelashes at him.

She was smart to notice there was nothing on the tray to whip up for dessert. Little did she know, he'd arranged for a chocolate fondue to show up a bit later.

"I'm not sweet enough for you?" He grinned, but already knew the answer. His moods were far from sweet.

She slid out of her chair and sidled up to him. "Oh, you're plenty sweet. And I'll be indulging in that sweetness"—she leaned in and nibbled his earlobe— "a little later." She bit down, and the twinge of pleasure-pain shot straight to his cock. "On second thought, why don't we have a little taste test right now?"

She grabbed the champagne bottle and her glass, and walked over to the pillow bed. He couldn't tear his eyes away from the sexy sway of her hips.

That tiny red dress rode up her thighs and exposed the bottom of her ass cheeks when she bent over to set the champagne on the floor.

The hut had sliding shutters on three of its sides, and at that moment he was happy with his decision to keep only the main ones open. He didn't want anyone getting a glimpse of her perfection, or catching them in the act, because every movement was on purpose. She even spread her legs a little to give him an eyeful of the black lace that covered her.

"We're having mahi-mahi," he said, trying to distract himself so he wouldn't attack her on the spot. "With mango salsa."

He started dicing the mango. The sweet smell of the fruit and the fresh tomatoes he'd chopped earlier wafted up and infused his senses. But she was pulling out all the stops to turn later into right now.

He did his best not to look at her ass and focus on cutting up the mango and red onion for the salsa, but she made it difficult to concentrate. He probably shouldn't even be using a knife at the moment. He was liable to cut off one or more of his fingers. A trip to the emergency room was not how he wanted tonight to end.

"And pineapple fried rice."

In another predetermined move to get him hard—*mission accomplished*—she kneeled, then crawled across the giant pillow, turning to settle in the center with her back against the wall. She made no attempt to close her legs. They remained wide open for his viewing pleasure. She crooked her finger at him, begging him with her eyes to come over and ravage her.

But there was ample time tonight to do what they did best. First, he wanted to take their relationship to the next level. Wanted it to be built on something more than sex. Yes, once they set foot on home soil everything they had built here in Hawaii would end. But he needed to let her in and share this with her, because once they got home, he wouldn't be able to do it.

But then she traced her finger up the inside of her thigh. The knife he was holding dropped to the cutting board.

"You are so not playing fair."

She smiled coyly.

Well, two could play that game.

He strode over to her. His erection throbbed in his linen pants. His pulse had doubled, and he had no doubt that his need for her was written all over his face.

He dropped to the floor, his knees hitting the softness of the pillows. He crawled up her body, planting light kisses on her feet, her calves, her thighs. Tickling his nose along her warm, sweet skin until he was face-to-face with the sweetest part of her. She pulled up her dress so she could see what he was doing, exposing her entire lower half. He flicked out his tongue and ever so lightly grazed over the lace of her thong. She moaned, and her head fell back against the pillows.

"You're not hungry?" he whispered against her core.

She moaned again. "You're all the food I need."

He didn't stop there. His mouth moved up, pressing a kiss to her stomach, then the peak of each breast through her dress, until he reached more exposed skin. He laid open-mouthed kisses on the swell of her cleavage. He kissed her collarbone, her neck, her nose, and forehead. And finally, when she was panting and her fists were curled around the pillow under her, he placed his lips to hers. With the same rhythm, he ground his hips between her legs, letting her know just how hard, how ready, he was for her. And just when she whimpered into his mouth and reached for the fly of his pants, he retreated.

She whimpered again, not in ecstasy but frustration. Her bottom lip jutted out, and she looked up at him with disappointed eyes. "You're so mean."

He pressed one last kiss to her lips, then backed away from the bed, shifting his pants as he returned to the grill.

When the food was finally prepared, she moaned over every bite. Needless to say, between that and the way she'd teased him from the bed while he was cooking, he'd had an erection for the last hour.

He was on his third Jack and Coke. The more time that passed, the closer he got to having to start his confession. Telling her things he didn't really want anyone to know. But his brain had just the right amount of buzz going, and his nervousness settled more with every sip.

"Everything was so delicious. Thank you." She wiped her mouth gently with the white cloth napkin. "Not that I would expect anything less."

He dropped his gaze to the floor. He loved cooking,

loved making people happy with his food, but never knew what to do with the compliments.

This was the perfect opportunity. He had a solid buzz. Solid enough to drown out the persistent *don't do it* that pleaded with him from the back of his mind to keep her from knowing exactly why he was the way he was, and give her the opportunity to bolt. Or worse, feel sorry for him.

He needed more time. His heart pounded against his chest, and his arms were actually twitching with nervousness.

She backed her chair away from the table and locked her eyes on his. "I think it's time for me to thank the chef."

He gave her a smile. "You just did."

With a grin, she dropped to her knees and disappeared under the table.

"*Um…* I thought we could talk."

But she was intent on doing anything but talking. He heard the sound of his zipper lowering. He felt the warmth and moisture as she tongued him through his boxer briefs.

"Why? You never want to talk," she mumbled around licks to the tip of his cock, which was now exposed.

"I thought you wanted me to talk more—*oh, shit.*"

Her mouth engulfed his cock in one long swallow.

Fuck talking.

He groaned and surrendered. One hand found the long strands of her hair and guided her up and down his length.

Her mouth was good at so many things. Busting his balls. Arguing. Whispering words of encouragement she had no idea meant so much to him. But this— sucking his cock— was his favorite of all.

Suddenly, a loud voice burst through the hut. "Hey, Penn!"

Penn's head hit the table.

"Get out here, you two." Cole recognized the voice. It was Pete yelling from outside.

Penn laughed. "Sounds like my brother's already been drinking." She crawled out from under the table. "Which means... They've all been drinking." She grabbed the champagne from the table and took a swig straight from the bottle. "Better catch up."

"Hold on." Cole pushed away from the table and did up his pants.

He opened the door, and when he stepped out, Pete, Christine, Beth, Dave, Ian, and Cathy all stood at the bottom of the steps to the hut.

"How did you find us?" He hadn't mentioned anything to her family about where they'd be. Not only because he wanted them to be alone, but because he didn't want to force her to explain their relationship.

Dave smirked. "It's amazing what information you can get when you drop a fifty into someone's hand."

Jason was dead meat.

"What are you guys doing in there?" Cathy looked positively devious.

"We're..." He had no idea. His mind was completely blank. And thankfully, his cock was completely deflated. The moment he'd heard Pete's voice he'd gone soft.

"We're working." Penn to the rescue. "Cole's Boys and Girls Club launches just after we get home, so we're going over some last minute details."

"In a romantic hut on the water?" Beth didn't look convinced. She tapped her finger against the crease of her elbow where her arms were crossed over her chest.

"They...don't have a business center here," he blurted.

He knew that from the first day he'd gotten here when he felt guilty about leaving club business and was shocked to find out this place was just for fun. "The hut was the only space I could get where we could have room to work and not be disturbed."

He glanced over at Penn, who was still in the doorway, and she gave him the slightest nod in appreciation.

"Why's your hair messy, Penn?" Dave asked.

Shit.

Luckily, they didn't have to respond thanks to Cathy's excited outburst.

"We're going dancing," she said cheerfully. "Why don't you guys come?"

"We're kind of busy." He jerked a thumb back at the hut.

"Come on. How often are you going to be in Hawaii?" Christine said.

She had a point. Although the thought of dancing made Cole want to hurl, Penn loved getting out on a dance floor.

"Give us a minute," he said, resigned.

When he returned to Penn, she looked none too pleased. "What if I don't want to go dancing?"

"You love dancing."

"That's not what *they* think." She scrunched up her face and said in a mimicking tone, "Pennie doesn't dance."

He laughed. Okay. Now he actually wanted to go. "Come on. This is your opportunity to show them up. I know you've got moves."

On the dance floor and in the bedroom.

"But what about our special night?" She pouted.

He wasn't happy about the interruption, either. But it did give him more time to gather his thoughts. And his courage. Work out the best way to tell her about his past. He could use the extra time.

Besides, he'd wanted her to come out of her shell with her family all day, and this was a golden opportunity.

"I know you have a lot of moves you can show me on that dance floor. And frankly"—leaning down, he whispered in her ear—"if I can't have you rubbing up against me on that pillow, I'll take whatever rubbing I can get." He stood and pulled back his shoulders to gather his thoughts.

That was kind of dirty. Wasn't it?

"Thank you." Penn's eyes sparkled, that gorgeous cobalt blue color returning to mesmerize him. She stood, wrapping her arms around his neck. "You've made this trip so much easier."

"You might want to keep the thank-yous for later," he whispered, "when I'm fucking you under the moonlight."

That was definitely dirty.

Her eyes flared with desire. "Where did that come from?"

He leaned forward and rested his forehead against hers. "I have no idea." He pressed his lips to hers. "But you know you love it."

Love.

How the hell had that word snuck into his vocabulary? He didn't love Penn. He *couldn't* love Penn.

Could he?

She squeezed his hand. "Let's go show my family who doesn't have two left feet." Her lips curled up, making a face, but she relented. "But I'm bringing the champagne."

And she did.

The entire bottle.

Without a glass.

The drinking didn't stop on the beach on the way to the club. It happened outside the club. Inside the club. And on the dance floor. With the exception of Christine, they were all three sheets to the wind.

There were at least a hundred people in the club. It was sweaty and hot, but the perfect venue for them to get lost in each other, without thinking about the future.

But then a spotlight fell on their table, and the DJ walked out to the front of the stage that sat to the left of the dance floor. "Ladies and gentlemen, we've been asked to help out with a family rivalry." He pointed down at their table as the crowd hooted and hollered. "Pennie and Beth?" He waved his arm toward the stage. "Why don't you come up here?"

Penn went rigid beside him, a shocked expression replacing the contentedness that was there only a second ago.

"What the hell is going on?" she spat.

He looked around the entire table, from one sibling to the next, but they all looked at each other with confusion, except for Cathy, who laughed under her breath.

"Cathy, what did you do?" Penn yelled from her seat beside him. Her breath had picked up, and he noticed her foot tap in nervousness, making her leg move up and down rapidly.

Cathy shrugged, then sat back in her seat. "I thought it would be fun to see Miss Goodie-Two-Shoes shake her booty on stage." She waved a finger toward Penn.

Cole suppressed his laugh. Penn was anything but a goodie-two-shoes.

"What!" Penn shouted. "Do you hate me or something?" A small whimper escaped her mouth as she shook beside him in terror.

"Ian and I won't be winning anything this year." Cathy let out a gleeful noise. "I've got to get something out of it."

He'd always thought Cathy was nosy, maybe a little intrusive, but never vindictive. Alcohol really did show peoples' true colors.

"What do you say, ladies?" the DJ asked. The spotlight had gotten brighter, hotter, over their table, and Cole had to squint to make him out on stage. "Will we be judging a hula contest, or what?"

"Fuck. Fuck. Fuck," Penn mumbled beside him, not loud enough for anyone else to hear.

"Penn, you don't have to do this," he whispered from his seat.

She looked up at him, some of the nervousness disappearing when she looked into his eyes. He placed his hand on her thigh under the table, telling her without words that he was here if she needed him. Giving her the same silent support she'd always given him.

She smiled up at him and placed her hand over his. With a soft sigh, she whispered, "Be myself, right?"

He wanted to lean forward and rest his forehead on hers, kiss her, but he held back. Instead he mumbled, "You can do this."

With one forceful nod, she made her decision.

Penn slapped her hand on the table, grabbed one of the shots that had been placed at her seat while they were dancing, then picked up his and downed that one, too.

She looked at her sister-in-law and gave a cocky smile. "Put on your skirt, Beth. It's go time."

His stomach was in knots for her, but there was no way she would falter. Penn did everything with flying colors.

Dancing on stage would be no different. Plus, he already knew how good she could move.

This was her time to shine. To show her family just what she could do. And they would be proud of her. Embrace her with open arms.

Because that's what family did.

Chapter Eleven

Penn must have blacked out.

One minute she was at the table with her siblings having a great time, the next she was waiting backstage in a stupid grass skirt and coconut bra.

"Come on out here." The DJ beckoned them to center stage.

With a deep breath, she gathered all the courage she had, but she knew it wasn't going to be enough.

The crowd roared when they walked out on stage, and fear gripped her insides when she took her spot beside Beth. The music had been turned down significantly, and now all she heard was the buzz of the crowd.

Just great. Now you can hear every individual voice when they boo you off this fucking stage.

The DJ circled, giving them the once-over. "These are some good looking ladies."

He had his septum pierced, dark hair, and light brown

skin, and he was dressed in a Hawaiian shirt. "These ladies are going to hula for us, and we get to pick the winner. I think we can do that, right people?"

The onlookers went nuts. Luckily, the blinding lights from the stage made it almost impossible to distinguish people in the crowd, but it wasn't helping to keep down the two shots she'd just chugged before getting on stage.

"Cue the ukuleles." The DJ circled a theatrical finger and pointed to the AV guy at the back of the stage.

The soothing sounds of Hawaiian music filled the club. A healthy difference from the bass that had pumped through the sound system from the moment they'd arrived.

"Come on, Penn!" She heard Christine scream from below the stage. "You can do this."

She took three quick breaths, fisting her hands at her sides.

What the fuck was wrong with her? She could do this. She danced on tables for Christ's sake, but stick her in front of her family and suddenly she wanted to hide inside the wallpaper.

Penn moved her bare feet, transferring her weight from one foot to the other, and fluttered her arms at her sides. The coconut bra was tight around her torso, since she hadn't taken off her dress for fear of exposing her tattoo. The wood of the stage was slippery under her feet. It was probably her nervous sweat.

It took a few beats, but she finally got a rhythm. In her periphery, she noticed Beth dancing with the same soft movements. The noisy crowd urged her on, and she heard Cole shouting for her in the distance, anchoring her in the moment.

Then the lights dimmed, making it easier for her to see. Which made it infinitely worse. Now, with everyone's eyes on her, she felt paralyzed. She found Cole in the crowd and locked eyes with his. Screw this.

She couldn't do sexy. Not in front of her siblings.

But when she looked over at Beth, she had that look in her eye. She was looking to redeem herself.

Penn sighed. She had demanded that Cole put on his big boy pants if he wanted to play. She was going to have to listen to her own advice. Even if that advice meant shaking her groove thing and putting a small crack in the mold her family had squeezed her into.

Suddenly, the crowd erupted, and she turned. The blinding lights above returned, causing her to squint. But even with blurred vision, she'd recognize that silhouette anywhere.

Cole was making his way on stage.

To her right, Dave sidled up to Beth. When Cole's warm hand snaked up her back and gripped her shoulder, she melted into him.

Her heart swelled. Once again he'd come to save the day.

"I think we've just upped the ante, ladies and gentlemen." The DJ walked to the front of the stage. "We now have a couples contest."

"Cole?" she whispered, turning slightly so she could see his face. He stood behind her, most of his body covered by hers. "What are you doing?"

Their eyes met, and he gave her a look that screamed, "No fucking clue."

They were both floundering on this island, trying to shed some of the chains they'd brought with them from home. But he was here for her. He had come to this island *for her*.

"Sexy is your specialty," he whispered in her ear. "Let's show them what you got."

Over the last few days she'd seen him blossom and come out of his shell. And his unconditional support and concern for her well-being was overwhelming. He had been right. She needed to show her family exactly the woman she'd become. Because she was awesome. Successful. Happy. Proud of the woman she saw in the mirror every day. And even more, she loved the woman she saw in Cole's eyes.

"Are you ready?" The DJ stood at the front of the stage with his back to the roaring crowd. "The sexiest couple wins."

Of all people, it had been Cole Murphy that had forced her to realize she could be herself, that she *should* be herself, because she was enough.

She switched her position with Cole, taking her place at his back. She wove her hands through his arms and staked her claim, one hand gripping his hard pec, the other braced against the smooth ripple of his abs.

"Just go with the flow," she whispered.

He turned his head. "If I go with the flow, I'm liable to get arrested for indecent exposure."

She giggled. "Then I'll just make sure to cover your front with my back."

He shook his head, letting it fall forward. "That might be worse."

Her laughter was drowned out when the music changed from ukuleles to a slow, sensual bass that was perfect for what she had in mind. She loved dancing. Loved moving her body in the most torturous way. And she was going to torture Cole.

She teased him. Made him moan. She wasn't thinking

about the crowd full of people behind her. She didn't even care that her brother and sister-in-law were right beside them. Right now, it was just the two of them.

Making sure one part of her body remained connected with his at all times, she stepped in front, threading her arms around his neck. Her hips pressed into him, and she undulated rhythmically, moving her body from side to side. His hands found her hips, his fingers digging into her through the fabric of her dress.

With a grin, she turned, pressing her backside into him. His low grunt kicked up her movements. Letting her head fall forward, she bent at the waist, then wiggled her ass. She was happy for her decision to wear heels tonight. She needed the height. Needed it to remain in position when she bent over and placed one hand on the stage.

She felt the fabric of his pants against her ass cheeks. Her dress must have risen with her movements. When she turned her head, she watched as he held up his hands, fingers twitching to touch her bare skin. But he didn't.

"I think it's getting hot in here." The DJ whistled into the microphone.

She was having fun. Something she never had to *try* to have when she was away from her family.

She straightened and threw her head back, her hair hitting Cole in the face. She craned her neck and looked up at him. She wanted to kiss him. She wanted to devour him right on this stage. But she'd keep it PG-13. Although with the amount of thrusting and grinding, maybe she was running into R rated territory.

He groaned into her ear. "You're making it really hard for me not to throw you over my shoulder and find the nearest dark space."

"Oh…" She wiggled out of his arms and danced slowly around his body, letting her fingers drag across his chest. She settled flush against his back. "I think it's already hard."

She took slow, deliberate steps as she made her way back to stand in front of him. She swept her hair up with both hands, exposing her neck to fresh air, then let it fall over her shoulders.

Sweat had broken out across her skin. It had already been hot in the club, but now that she was one step away from dry humping him in public…

"I think we have a winner, ladies and gentlemen."

When Penn looked over, both Dave and Beth had stopped dancing.

The DJ grabbed Cole's wrist and thrust his hand into the air. Cole mimicked his actions and did the same with Penn, raising her hand in victory.

Beside her, she heard Beth curse. When she stole a look, her lips were drawn in a thin line, and she was fisting her hands at her sides.

A flash of heat engulfed her. She bit her thumbnail as a blush settled into her cheeks. She'd just humped Cole in public. She'd just done sexy…in front of her siblings.

It could have been a hell of a lot sexier. But this was a huge baby step in the right direction. And she couldn't have done it without Cole.

He had gotten on that plane to help her win that trophy. But she knew now it was far more than that. Destiny had brought him to this island. This was the universe's way of telling her to make a change.

They made their way backstage, letting a disgruntled

Beth sulk her way back to the table with Dave.

Penn pulled Cole to a stop and wrapped her arms around him. They only had a moment before they'd be in public again.

"Thank you." She kissed him softly, quickly. "That felt really good."

"You did all the work." His big hands slid down her back and rested just above her ass. "I just stood there and tried not to get an erection."

She laughed. "Which you failed miserably."

He kissed her forehead. "That I did."

When they made their way off stage, they returned to her siblings, most of them with disapproving looks, at their table.

"Where did you learn to do that?" Cathy asked, forcing everyone at the table to stare in their direction.

Penn suppressed her amusement. Cathy had tried to get the last laugh, thinking Penn would fall flat on her face. But she hadn't. Imagine if she'd gone full Penn on that stage. They'd all be stunned silent.

"I thought it was hot," Christine said, then took a sip of water.

Ian cleared his throat. "You sure know how to get Pennie to come out of her shell." He looked over at Cole, who simply smiled.

"Penn doesn't really have a shell."

She knew he'd been trying the whole time he'd been here to drop hints, to get her family to realize she wasn't the same little girl. But they were so oblivious, or so intent on keeping her in the box, they just didn't see it.

"Really, Pennie." Cathy leaned over the table, lowering

her voice as best she could over the music. "Do you think Dad would approve of you dancing like that? All you were missing was the pole."

Anger bubbled inside her. Of course she would bring Dad into it, and she had no doubt one of them would rat her out tomorrow morning at breakfast. But she had nothing to be ashamed of.

She smacked the table in frustration. "Get over it, Cathy. I won."

"Good thing you didn't become a teacher like Dad wanted, Penn," Dave said, twisting his beer bottle in his hand on the table. "Clearly you're not right for the job."

Just because she liked to grind on the dance floor didn't mean she'd be a bad teacher, a bad influence. She just didn't *want* to be a teacher.

"Are you sure you two aren't dating?" Beth cocked her head to the side, her eyes darting between them. "You look pretty familiar with each other."

Shit. Her decision to crack the mold was backfiring. Beth was getting suspicious.

What did you expect? Your ass was all over his dick.

"Women all over the world sexy-dance with guys they aren't dating." They were all getting suspicious. She couldn't miss the side-eyed glances, the rolling eyes every time she tried to defend their non-couple status.

Her heart sank. She'd shown them barely ten percent of what she was like at home, and this was what she got.

It wasn't worth it.

"No wonder you have so much free reign at your job." Beth wasn't letting up. "It must be nice —"

"I think we need to get back to work." Cole stood,

pushing his chair back.

She sucked in a steadying breath. Cole's timing was impeccable. He was one step away from clinching the knight in shining armor title.

She scrambled up from her seat and sidled closer to him. She couldn't help it. She needed his warmth, his familiarity, that something he gave her that she just couldn't put her finger on.

Without even saying good night to her siblings, they made their way along the beach toward the hut. She held her stilettos in her other hand and let the water wash over her feet with each rise of the tide. Cole had rolled up his pants and carried his shoes, too.

She took in a deep breath, letting the fresh, spicy air fill her senses. *This* moment was perfect. She felt free. Safe. Somehow saying thank you to Cole didn't seem enough.

"The first time I ever saw the ocean was when I was sixteen years old," he said, his voice low, barely a whisper against the sound of the waves.

She looked up at him in surprise. Had he really just revealed something about himself out of the blue? If this was his attempt at distracting her from the disaster that had just happened in that club, then it was working.

"Yeah?" she said softly. She didn't want to push him. She was there to listen.

"Vivian took Finn, Neil, and me to the beach for two weeks the summer before Jack came to live with us." He looked over at her. "Pretty pathetic, huh?"

She shook her head. "Not at all."

"I had a lot of firsts while living with Vivian." His fingers brushed hers at their sides, sending an electric sizzle up her arm that settled in her chest, but she pulled away immediately. "First live professional sporting event." He glanced at her. "Hockey, of course. First Christmas tree that wasn't a meaningless token given by our group home. One that actually had presents under it." He gave a sad laugh. "With a real tag that had my name on it."

No wonder he was so broody. He'd spent most of his life with no love. Even her crazy family showed affection once in a while. She had expected his story to be sad, but this was heartbreaking.

Her fingers itched to reach out and touch him, but she held still. Their touching had to be reserved for inside the hut. She hadn't just gone through the stress of denying a romantic relationship to blow it all now.

"How did Vivian find you?"

"She visited our group home—the one I grew up in, along with Finn, Veronica, and her brother, Mark. By then, Mark and Veronica were living two hours away with a nice family. So, it was just Finn and me left there with a heap of other kids. Vivian took pity on us, I guess, and became our new foster parent."

Vivian Madewood had been a saint.

"Neil wasn't so happy about us moving in. He'd had a chip on his shoulder for a while."

"A chip on his shoulder? Neil?" She faked a gasp.

He laughed, and his teeth sparkled in the moonlight. She loved that smile. It always kicked up a flutter in her stomach.

The tiki torches that lined the boardwalk and stairs were burning brightly, guiding their way home. Only a few more steps to their hut.

"Penn?" he whispered beside her.

"Hmm?" She settled her gaze on the sand below, at her toes squishing against the abrasive grains.

"Thank you."

"Whatever for?" She looked up into his eyes. "I should be thanking you. What you did for me tonight—"

He pulled her to a stop, seriousness darkening his gaze. "I wanted to. I owe you." He shrugged. "I've been such a jerk for so long. Never giving you an inch. But you never gave up on me." He kissed her hair. "I've had a lot of fun with you this week, and guess what, the world didn't blow up without me watching over it."

She could scarcely believe her ears. She was so happy she thought she might float away. But she wasn't just happy with him; she was happy with herself.

"What *I* did tonight…" She looked up, biting her bottom lip. "Man, I'm going to catch a lot of shit for it tomorrow."

"Either way, you were great. You were…more like you." He reached out and brushed her hair away from her face.

Voices and laughter drifted from the resort. Lights twinkled in the distance as they stood on the path to their hut, sexual tension crackling between them.

"I should also thank you for pulling that stick out of my ass."

She beamed up at him. "It was my pleasure."

"Penn, I…"

She urged him on with a tilt of her head.

His eyes darkened in the moonlight. "I want you."

She smiled and whispered, "I want you, too."

With every moment that passed, with every second they gazed into each other's eyes, her heart beat faster. Her stomach fluttered so badly it felt as though it would burst out of her skin. It was the greatest feeling, and she never wanted it to end.

Maybe it doesn't have to.

She had planned to sell her qualifications to the Madewood boys hard, but what if she sat back and did…nothing? How likely would it be then that she'd be considered for a spot on the board?

When Cole reached out to grab her, she stepped away, looking both ways down the beach. She jerked her chin toward the hut. They stood silent for a beat, and then both of them laughed, bolting for the staircase that led to their private paradise. She stumbled a few feet from the hut, but she used a rock formation that housed a pond with bright orange fish to steady herself.

He was up the stairs before her, fumbling inside his pants pocket for the key card. She rested her hand against the shutter, trying her best to catch her breath, but Cole wasn't interested in letting her rest. His hand clasped around the back of her head and brought her mouth to his. Now that they were out of sight, she sank into the kiss. Into the feel of his lips and tongue, and that special way he made her feel with all her senses.

He pressed her into the wall, his grinding erection a surprise against her stomach.

"Inside." She sucked in gulping breaths. "Now," she demanded.

He unlocked the shutters, and they slipped inside. She wasted no time undoing the buttons of his shirt and parting the edges. She ran her hands through the sprinkle of chest hair, loving the way it felt on her hands, the rough contrast to the firm smoothness of the rest of him.

He locked the shutters, keeping out everything that threatened to ruin them. Real life had no place on this island, in this hut. And she was going to enjoy this fantasy for the short time they had left together.

She led him over to the pillow bed and pushed at his chest. "Sit."

He stumbled back, his butt hitting the center of the pillow.

When he had settled and crossed his legs, she smiled down at him. "How about a dance?"

Her mouth watered at the sight of the wedge of tanned skin between the open sides of his shirt, wanting nothing more than to lick her way from his nipples to his cock.

She didn't have any music, but it didn't matter because she was too hyped to actually dance. Instead, she slowly and sensually removed her clothing, one item at a time, starting with undoing the belt at her waist, then the zipper in back. The dress fell to the floor and she stepped out of it. She walked up and stopped at the edge of the pillow bed, widening her stance.

He rubbed at his cock through his pants, watching her with half-lidded eyes. She stepped onto the mattress, and he stretched out his legs between hers as she came closer and closer, until the juncture of her thighs was inches from his face. She spread her legs and lowered her body, letting her core slide down his chest. Just before touching his erection, she eased back up. She teased him like that a few times, sometimes with a hand to his face, sometimes with a lick to his lips. With each movement, the flimsy lace of her thong scratched against her clit.

When she was satisfied he'd been tortured enough, she

stood and turned, again putting her feet to either side of his legs. After bending over, she grabbed her ankles.

"Take out your cock," she commanded, looking at him through her legs.

He smiled and did as he was told. "You want this?" He rubbed at the hard length.

She'd never wanted anything more in her life.

"Then you should already be ready for me." He stroked her backside, kneading and squeezing what she knew was his favorite body part.

He gripped the waist of her thong and slowly, torturously, pulled it over her hips and down her thighs. She lifted a foot so it pooled around one ankle.

Reaching out, he slipped his hand between her folds. No teasing. No torturing. He took exactly what he wanted. She hissed when he slipped a finger inside.

He groaned. "That's my girl." He fumbled in his pants for a condom and put it on. "Sink down on me." He fisted his erection, holding it out for her.

She squatted and rested her palms on the floor in front of her. He positioned his cock, and that first touch of the tip at her entrance was absolute magic.

He guided her down with his hands on her ass, inch by inch, letting his smooth length penetrate her body. An invasion so necessary, so not enough…

"Slow. That's— *Fu-uck*…"

She engulfed him. All of him. But he didn't let her linger. He pumped her up and down, up and down, building a steady rhythm, a slow burn tingling all over her body.

"That feels so good." She dropped her knees to the pillow. "So fucking good." Leaning forward, she moved up and down on his cock, taking over the rhythm.

He filled her so completely. She felt him in every nerve ending. She was on fire, smoldering with need and desire. For him.

For Cole.

Soft curses escaped his mouth the faster she bounced on his cock.

"I love your ass. It's fucking perfect." He smacked it and sent a shiver to her clit.

She bounced harder, the slapping sounds of skin against skin echoing through the hut. She locked her gaze on the bottle of Jack Daniels, took in her surroundings, maintained a keen focus, and stayed determinedly in the moment. She never wanted to forget this moment—the feelings that shot her physical pleasure to unchartered territory. But she'd keep those feelings safely hidden where he would know nothing about them.

She was staring down the barrel of a life-changing realization. And that alone was enough to tip her over the edge.

But he thrust up, harder this time, hitting a sweet spot she hadn't even known existed. Her body tensed, and she tipped over the precipice. She fell headlong into the colorful abyss and laid her heart on the table, letting him claim it with every quiver and throb of her orgasm.

He pushed her off, and his cock slapped against his stomach. He pressed his fingers to her folds, massaging the last thrums of her orgasm.

"Turn around baby," he whispered. "I want to see you."

Her body limp, she climbed over his legs and straddled him, face-to-face.

She rubbed herself along his cock, letting his hard shaft

peek out, then disappear between her folds. Her body reacted immediately to the friction. It hadn't taken long for her to jump to the edge again.

She rested her forehead against his. "On a normal day, you make my heart race so fast I can't catch my breath, and I just want to jump out of my skin. But now…" She clasped his face and pressed her lips to his, sucking and licking in uncontrollable need.

But she stifled her emotions. This was about fucking. Temporary. Fucking.

Her orgasm had been spectacular. She'd thought she'd been sated. But instead, she burned for more. For something stronger, harder, more consuming.

"I need more. Give me more."

She slipped him inside and moved, giving him the up and down friction he needed to get off. The closeness of their bodies also gave her the steady grind of her clit against his pelvis that she needed to soar a second time.

Somehow he met her with thrusts of his own, pressing deeper, harder. And it was exactly what she wanted. She wanted him inside her, joined so close she didn't know where he stopped and she began.

That was the way it had always been with Cole, body and soul. From the very first time they'd met she'd known they had a connection.

Her breath hitched, and she couldn't catch it. Until he kissed her—like he was the very breath she needed to survive.

"Look at me," he commanded.

She opened her eyes. "Cole, I—"

Don't say it. Don't you dare say it.

"Cole, I'm…coming."

This time, her pleasure didn't explode, it consumed. It washed over her like a wave, crashing from the top of her head down to the tips of her toes. It engulfed her in everything that was Cole.

Her head dropped and rested on his shoulder. They stayed in each other's embrace, their chests rising and falling with deep, heavy breaths.

Tomorrow was the scavenger hunt. The only reason he'd shown up on this island. But somehow, they'd managed to change the game and ended up giving in to the sexual tension that had smoldered between them for three years.

Coming out of her shell tonight with her family, even the slightest bit, had backfired. It had proved that she could never truly be herself with them. Despite feeling stifled, she enjoyed the relationships she had with her family, and pretending to be a toned-down version of herself for a few days each year was worth keeping those relationships intact.

Once the trophy was successfully in her hands, Cole would have fulfilled his duty, and they could return home, back to their normal roles.

She wasn't going to rest until that spot on the board of directors was hers. She needed her head in the game, not on Cole's skills in the bedroom. A temporary fling on vacation was one thing. But she had too much pride to let a permanent relationship dictate her career. She was never going to let that happen again.

Chapter Twelve

Cole put on his flip-flops and headed down to the dining room to meet Penn and her family.

They had showered and dressed separately this morning for the first time since they'd agreed to take their relationship to the bedroom. Penn had been a nervous wreck when they'd woken in the hut. She'd barely spoken to him, tension and nervousness overwhelming her to the point of distraction. He knew she was terrified over what was going to transpire this morning, afraid her siblings would tell her parents about her inappropriate dancing. After what he'd seen last night at the table, he knew it was a distinct possibility.

But Penn wasn't the only one in need of distance. Last night had been intense on so many levels. Not just the sex.

It was cooler this morning with the sun hiding behind a set of clouds as he wound through the pathway through the pools to the main building. For the first time since he'd arrived, he didn't have a light sheen of sweat dampening his skin.

He'd gotten on stage and put on a show. In public where anyone could have snapped a picture. His desperate need to defend and protect Penn had become overwhelming, and he'd proven to himself that he could be more than just a moody, broody, pain in the ass.

But maybe chickening out last night was a blessing in disguise. He'd gotten so caught up in his lust for her that he had convinced himself telling Penn the truth about his past was a good thing. The last thing he needed was to burden her with the knowledge, to have her thinking about it while they worked together. He wanted no one's pity. Especially when it came to Penn.

Sex had quickly become his go-to means of connecting with her. He could say so much more with his cock than his words ever could. And now that they were leaving in three days, that would have to be enough.

She was chewing on her thumbnail when he arrived at the buffet. He wasn't surprised to see that she'd gone back to wearing a one-piece bathing suit.

The spot beside her was empty, and he took his seat, immediately noticing the sly grins and expressions of distaste from her siblings through the entire meal. He didn't reach out and touch her, even though he wanted to. He kept his distance.

"Good morning, everyone," Cole said, giving them his best fake smile.

"Mrs. Foster and I were just getting a detailed account of what you kids were up to last night."

He tensed. Was he talking about dancing? Or did he somehow see them in the hut?

He glanced over at Penn.

"I didn't raise you to be inappropriate in public, Pennelope. Family vacation is no time for indulging in..." Her father's jaw twitched. "Sexcapades."

"What's a sexcapade?" Sarah asked, once again dancing in her seat to her own music.

"Really, Penn." Cathy glared at her from across the table, rubbing her hand over Sarah's hair. "See what you've done?"

He was shocked at the behavior of Penn's family. He had been so adamant that if she let down her guard and showed them her true self, they would accept her just as she was. He had been terribly wrong.

He hated seeing her upset. He hated seeing her trapped inside her shell. And this morning, he couldn't help but feel somewhat responsible because he'd pushed her to give it a try.

Breakfast was tense and mostly silent. Penn didn't look up from her plate once.

When breakfast was over, they all met in the hotel lobby where Harold handed out the lists for the scavenger hunt. There were twenty items needed for a perfect score, including a stamped card from the water sport rental hut, a receipt from the surf shop, and a napkin from every bar and restaurant in the hotel. In addition, there was one bonus item—a selfie with "something that swims." Weird. Were they supposed to swim out and catch a dolphin?

He whispered to Penn, "May I say, the lengths your father goes to arrange these daily challenges are mind-boggling."

"No doubt he's been scoping this place out since we arrived." She looked over the scavenger hunt list. "One year we actually had to make a dream-catcher, and the winner was picked by one of our neighbors."

Her father went over the rules. Teams could split up. All items had to be collected and handed in at their designated spot. The team with the best time and all the items won. Bringing in the bonus item shaved ten minutes off the team's time. Simple as that.

"Penn, are you—"

She placed her hand on his arm. "Whatever just happened…" She shrugged. "It happened. I'm here to win the trophy. That's all that matters."

He knew it mattered, what had happened last night and this morning at breakfast. But he wasn't going to push her. Instead, he'd do what he came here to do. He'd help her win that trophy.

"Dave and Beth, Cole and Pennie." Her father looked between the four of them. "You're tied with two wins each. Whoever has the best time with all the items, wins the cup."

After a quick glance at the list, Cole asked, "So what's our strategy?"

Penn sucked in a deep breath. She seemed to have cooled down and relaxed at little. "Divide and conquer. We meet back here when we're done." He loved the determined set to her jaw. His Penn was back.

She's not yours.

She ripped the paper in two. "Here's your half."

Excitement built as he grasped the paper. Oh, yeah. They were so going to win this.

With a high-five, they took off, each needing to collect ten items.

Cole raced through the hotel compound at break-neck

speed. He grabbed a rental receipt from the boat hut on the beach, a menu from the steakhouse at the far end of the grounds, and a brochure from the parasailing kiosk in the hotel lobby. As fast as he could, he collected twelve items on the list.

Almost an hour later, he was on his last item—a bar of lavender soap. He raced across the lobby to the elevators. After waiting ten seconds for it to arrive, he ran around and took the stairs two at a time down to the lower level. He rushed past groups of shoppers, trying not to mow anyone down.

Just before he reached the spa, he saw Christine and Pete. They were huddled together against the wall, giggling and smiling as they whispered to each other with contented gleams in their eyes. One of Pete's forearms rested on her shoulder, his other hand resting on her belly.

It was a Kodak moment. They looked so happy, lost in each other, as if the rest of the world didn't exist.

Cole knew exactly how it felt. Every single minute he'd spent with Penn this week, he'd been completely lost in her. Time had stood still. His brothers, his restaurant, the Boys and Girls Club... None of that mattered. He'd lived for their every moment together—for her reassuring smiles, her ability to ease his tension, and the special way she brought him out of his shell. He had tried to do the same thing for her, but it had proved to be more complicated than he'd anticipated. But most of all, he lived for the way she made him feel like the best version of himself, even if deep down, he knew his best self wasn't someone she could ever love.

Penn was all that mattered.

Someone bumped him from behind, and he was yanked

back to the present. He shook his head. *Damn.* He needed to concentrate on the task at hand, not moon over his lover. If they didn't win this trophy, he sure as hell wasn't going to see any more of her pretty smiles coming his way.

He hurried into the spa and headed for the desk. The receptionist greeted him as he approached, but when he practically skidded into the counter, she backed away.

"May I hel—"

"I need a bar of lavender soap." He drummed his fingers on the marble. "Like, right away."

She fetched one from the display, and he grabbed it, slammed down a twenty, and took off to her bewildered look.

He'd completed his half of the list in under an hour. Not bad, if he did say so himself. But when he arrived at the designated meeting area, Penn was nowhere to be seen.

He sent a text letting her know he'd finished his part of the list. When two minutes had gone by with no response, he sent another text.

Still no word.

He was getting worried.

He did a three-sixty spin for the twelfth time, trying to spot her in the crowd of people. He shouldn't leave in case she showed up, but what if something had happened to her?

To his relief, his name was shouted across the lobby.

He turned and saw her running toward him, her beach bag flapping behind her.

"Cole!"

She didn't slow down, but she barreled into him, almost tackling him to the floor. She panted like she'd just completed a marathon.

"Did you get all your items?" he asked.

She nodded and choked down a breath. "Yes."

Hallelujah. Without knowing how far along the other teams were, he had no idea if they were ahead of the winning time or behind it. But he guessed that was the point of different meeting places.

"You?" she asked.

He held up his bag. "Locked and loaded. I might have trampled a few kids to get them."

"That's my man." She backhanded his chest in appreciation, then looked at her watch. "I know how to get the bonus item."

He groaned. "Please don't tell me we're wrestling a dolphin." He had no idea how they were going to take a selfie with something that swam.

She laughed. "No. I've thought of something much easier and faster. The hut."

Her eyes were wide and excited, as if he was supposed to know what she was talking about. But he had no idea where she was going with this.

"The koi pond by the hut." Her eyebrows lifted. "Koi fish? Something that swims?"

He stepped back and surveyed her confident stance. "You're brilliant."

"Get your cell phone ready, Murphy." She winked. "We're going koi hunting."

Four minutes later, there was one more selfie added to his photo gallery.

They raced back to the finish line—the concierge desk in the hotel lobby. A familiar face was waiting for them when they arrived.

"Jason. Good to see you." Cole held out his hand and smiled.

"Mr. Murphy. I trust your scavenger hunt was successful."

"You know it."

He wondered if this was the most unusual request Jason had ever gotten while working at the hotel. He hoped Harold had tipped him well. "Please tell me this is the first time you've ever had to be the point person for a family scavenger hunt."

Jason laughed. "You'd be surprised what people ask you to do." He checked his watch and wrote down the time on a piece of paper. "Eleven forty-three."

"How did we do? Did we win?" Penn asked anxiously.

Jason shook his head. "Sorry, Miss Foster, you know I can't tell you that."

"I know. I just— I'm really nervous." She placed the bag filled with their items on the counter. "It's all here."

"And the bonus item?" Jason asked expectantly.

Cole pulled out his phone and showed him the selfie.

"Excellent." Jason smiled and noted it on the paper. "Thank you. I wish you the best of luck." He picked up their bag, placed the piece of paper inside, and walked off with it.

"We make a damn good team," Cole said proudly.

Penn sagged against the counter. Cole rubbed his hand up and down her back, trying to reassure her. "Now, all we have to do is wait for the results."

She nodded. "I really need to know if we won."

The official winner wouldn't be announced until dinner. *Tomorrow*. He needed to do something that would take her mind off it. Something fun to pass the time.

He leaned in and whispered in her ear, "Why don't we

go back to your room, and I can practice my dirty talk?"

She looked up, desire dancing in her gaze.

He was on top of the world right now. And nothing, not even if they came in last place, was going to ruin that.

"I am your willing guinea pig." She turned and wrapped her arms around his body, then rested her chin on his chest.

For the next twenty-four hours, he had Penn all to himself. And heaven help him, there was nowhere else he'd rather be.

Chapter Thirteen

Penn spent the next twenty-four hours with Cole in her room.

Room service sated their hunger, and Cole's hard cock satisfied her other hunger—the one that needed him desperately. The hunger she didn't think would ever be sated.

Yesterday, he'd given her the best opportunity she'd ever had of winning the Foster Cup. He had sacrificed his own work, his life at home, to be here for her. As if he really loved her.

But that was impossible. Cole Murphy wasn't the falling-in-love type. And tomorrow, when they packed up and left Hawaii, she would have to face reality and fall back into their familiar rhythm of friends and coworkers. She didn't have the luxury of screwing up her job. If she'd learned anything on this trip, it was that she needed to keep the people and spaces that allowed her to be herself close. She never thought she'd find a job where she'd have a hand in helping hundreds of people every year *and* be appreciated for her candor, enthusiasm, and occasional lack of propriety. But her job with the Madewood family was just that—a space where she could be herself.

But she wouldn't worry about that now. They still had one more night in paradise.

An hour before the award dinner, they showered and dressed in casual clothes. They planned to go to the beach after dinner to find a secluded spot and… Well, they'd just continue what they had been doing in their room.

Cole left ahead of her for dinner. He was too nervous, wearing a path in the floor from his pacing. So, she asked him to save them seats.

Just as she walked out of her hotel room, her phone buzzed in her purse. When she glanced at the screen, Sterling's face smiled back at her.

She swiped the screen and answered her call, but didn't even get in a greeting.

"I've been texting you all day!" Sterling's voice was a few octaves higher than usual.

"Sorry." She really wasn't. Ignoring Sterling's texts meant she was preoccupied with Cole. "I've been…busy."

Sterling made a playfully disgusted noise. "I don't want to know."

"How do you even know what I'm referring to?" Penn switched the phone to her opposite hand, then pressed the button to call the elevator.

"I know you." Sterling had a weird tone to her voice, and it was way too serious for her liking. "Which is why you need to hear what I have to say before it's too late."

"Too late for what?" The elevator dinged. "You're being

really cryptic."

"I overheard a conversation between Jack and Neil. They were discussing the vacant spot on the board."

With one foot inside the elevator, Penn froze. And waited.

Why had her best friend decided this was the best moment to go mute?

"And...?" she squealed into the phone, stepping back, narrowly missing the elevator doors crushing her.

"I might have heard your name come up as a replacement."

Her stomach flipped. "Get out!" she yelled. Leaning against the wall, she rested her head against it. "Are you sure? Me? Were there other names?" So many questions ran through her brain.

"I didn't hear them mention anyone else, but I don't know. They could have had other discussions."

This was insane. She might actually get what she'd wanted all along. She might finally—

Her chest tightened, and the excited feeling in her stomach churned into something sour. If she was on the board, then what she had with Cole absolutely had to stop. In spite of the tiny hope that fluttered in her chest every time she thought about things working out differently.

Her hesitance could only mean one thing. Maybe getting a spot on the board might not be everything she'd ever wanted.

Penn ended her call with Sterling and made her way to the restaurant. They were still in Hawaii. Still in the little bubble they'd made for themselves, and until they broke through, she wasn't going to think about the consequences of what a spot on the board might mean.

At the entrance to the dining room, she spotted Cole and her father.

She stopped dead in her tracks when she saw the look on her father's face and the rigid way he stood in front of Cole—the classic Sergeant Foster stance that had his shoulders pulled back and his hands clasped behind his back.

When she was within earshot, she heard her father say, "I'm just going to come out and say it." He glared at Cole. "I think you're a bad influence on my daughter."

That was preposterous. Penn had veered off the path of so-called appropriate behavior long ago.

She couldn't see Cole's expression because his back was to her. But her father's hadn't changed. He still looked pissed. And didn't that just make her retreat into the twelve-year-old girl who wanted nothing more than to please him.

She stalked up to the two men. "What's going on?" Her voice was meek, wavering.

"You've been avoiding the family," her father said between gritted teeth.

"We've…uh…"

She couldn't exactly say she'd been fucking Cole's brains out. Or that he was fucking hers. In the grand scheme of things… There had been lots of fucking all over her hotel room.

And maybe the bathroom.

Cole crossed his arms over his chest. "It seems your father thinks I'm a bad influence on you."

He seemed to be taking the criticism in stride.

"Of course you are." Her father glared. "My daughter is veering a long way from being the role model I raised her to be." His frown deepened. "The only explanation is your presence in her life."

"Forgive me for saying so, sir." Cole stood straighter. She was glad that he was aware enough not to touch her, to not show any type of affection whatsoever. "But I don't think you know your daughter at all."

Shit. Shit. Shit. Now Cole was going to rat her out. Had she stumbled into some sort of twilight zone?

"We should probably get into the buffet. Everyone's waiting for us," she interrupted. This was ridiculous.

"With all due respect, your daughter isn't the good girl you think she is. That is— " He regrouped. "She *is* a good girl, a great girl, but not the timid wallflower you've all made her out to be. And I, for one, admire that kind of strength and confidence. Penn's audacity is what I love most about her."

Her breath hiccupped, and she glanced up at him, but he kept his eyes on her father.

Love.

He'd just said *love*. And that he loved her non-good girl behavior. Her mind whirled. How could that be?

"I'm her father." Harold pointed at Cole's chest and loomed over the two of them in an intimidation tactic. "Are you trying to tell me that you know my daughter better than I do? Better than the man who taught her to ride a bike? To skate? To shoot hoops? To— "

"Yes. In fact, I do." Cole's face and body language were unflinching. He was playing the intimidator as well as her father. "When was the last time you actually sat down and talked to her?"

Her eyes widened, and her head spun even more. Cole was defending her. Again. He was by her side again. And she was just standing here saying nothing.

Her father bristled like a porcupine. "You've got a lot of nerve, young man. We may not be rich or famous, but we are a *family*, and we love each other no matter what."

A half-laugh, half-scoff shot out of Cole's mouth. "Yeah? That's also what I thought families did." He slid his arm around her shoulders, and she nestled into his protection. "Until I met yours."

"What is that supposed to mean?" After a moment of sputtering, he looked over at her and barked, "He's turning you against us."

She forced herself to respond. "I…"

She looked up at Cole. He urged her on with a nod, but she had nothing. He had just stuck his neck out for her, and she didn't even have enough courage to stick up for herself. Or for him.

"Harold, dear. Everyone is waiting." Her mother placed her hand gently on her father's arm, without even looking at him. She was staring right at Penn.

"I'm not fin—"

"Yes, you are." Her mom glared at her dad. It was… weird. Margot Foster *never* came between the Sergeant and an argument. "We have to announce the winner."

She tugged on his arm, her father letting out a disgruntled huff. But he took one more moment to stare down Cole, who gave it back to him in return.

When it was just the two of them, she hung her head.

"He shouldn't have said any of those things. I'm sorry," she said. "I should have—"

"I never thought I'd say this, but I miss your big mouth. I hate seeing you like this." He feathered his fingers through her hair, but she shrugged away. "Christ, Penn."

Tears stung behind her eyelids, but she blinked them away. She would not cry. She would not let the words of this man affect her so deeply. Because once they got back home, she might have to make a choice. And the odds were, that choice wouldn't include being with Cole.

Cole showing up in Hawaii had been the best thing to ever happen to her. And maybe, when they untangled themselves from between the bed sheets and went back to their regular, non-sexual lives, their friendship would be stronger because of it. But until then…

She had a trophy to win.

They walked, out of sync, into the dining room. Cole lagged two steps behind. Despite the edge between them, she wasn't going to let the confrontation ruin dinner.

She and Cole had totally kicked scavenger hunt ass. Kicked it right in the tuckus. He sat beside her, a cocky grin curving his mouth. The fact that he was here, supporting her, meant more to her than…well, than the trophy.

And you didn't have his back.

She looked around the table. Ian's arm was draped across his wife's shoulders, his hand absently rubbing her arm. Dave was pounding back a beer with a big smile on his face because he assumed, as he had for the last five years, he and Beth had won. And then there was Pete. Who was neither here nor there when it came to family competitions, but that didn't mean he didn't try his best. He just didn't throw it in anyone else's face. Which she appreciated.

But at the end of the day, they were her brothers, her ultimate competition, and she'd set out this year to beat them any way she could. In a few minutes she'd be holding that cup, a winner in their eyes for the very first time. Hopefully, overshadowing every stupid thing she'd done on this trip.

Cole's phone beeped inside his jacket pocket. She'd asked him to leave it in the room. As he pulled it out, she frowned. Cell phones at the table were a Foster no-no.

"Put that away," she whispered. He gave her a look.

The moment she saw the twitch in Cole's jaw, she knew. Something wasn't right.

"Something more interesting than this table, Mr. Murphy?" her father asked.

Cole had embarrassed him outside the restaurant. She knew his disapproving tone was a way to regain some of his control.

But by the look in Cole's eyes, there *was* something more interesting going on. The only question was whether it was a good interesting or a bad interesting. He shook it off and slunk back into his seat, mouthing, "Sorry."

When the waiter had taken their orders, Penn couldn't stand the awkward silence at the table. The tension between her and Cole was palpable, and she wanted to get down to business. "Can you just give me the cup now, so we can end this?"

"What makes you think you won?" Dave muttered.

"Because I got the bonus item—a selfie with a koi fish. Did any of you?" She crossed her arms over her chest and scanned their faces. She didn't think so.

Her father looked at her with sympathy. "I'm afraid you didn't win."

She stared at him blankly. "I'm sorry, what?" She did *not* just hear that.

"Yes!" Beth celebrated with a fist pump.

Oh, *hell*, no. "How is that possible? We made great time."

"And we got the selfie," Cole interjected. By the look of shock on his face, he couldn't believe it, either.

She'd *felt* the win, deep in her bones.

"Dave and Beth still had a better time, even when I subtracted the ten minutes," her father explained.

"But—"

Dave jumped up and hugged his father with one arm and his wife with the other.

"But we got the selfie," Penn mumbled under her breath.

Her father handed Dave and Beth the trophy.

Penn couldn't believe it.

She'd wasted Cole's time. She'd taken him away from the thing he loved the most. She'd even tried to show her family who she'd become.

It had all been for nothing. All of it.

"You need to be faster next time." Dave's winning grin made her sick. "Even with a ringer, you can't beat me, Pennie."

His phone beeped again, and he immediately took his phone out of his pocket and hid it under the table.

When he looked at the text, a funny look settled on his face. He'd been so happy all week that she'd almost forgotten what he looked like when sadness took over.

He blew out a heavy breath and stood. "I've got to go." He took off through the dining room, with no explanation.

"Cole?" She called after him, but he didn't turn around. Didn't stop.

She moved her chair out of the way to follow him, but she halted when her father's stern voice broke the silence of the table. "Not so fast, young lady."

Something had to be wrong. He wouldn't just leave like

this. She had to go to him. She had to be there for him. She owed him that much, considering she'd practically placed the noose around his neck when her father had confronted him before dinner.

"We're having a family dinner, Pennelope. Sit. Down."

All week Cole had stood by her side, and with one conversation, she'd knocked down all the progress they'd made in their relationship.

He'd walked away, because she'd given him no indication that she needed him.

But she *did* need him.

With a heavy sigh, she sunk into her chair and faced her family.

If there was ever a chance that this thing between her and Cole could blossom into something more, she'd just completely ruined it.

Chapter Fourteen

Cole ran on the treadmill, music blasting in his ears from his earbuds. He'd had to get out of that restaurant.

He wanted to punch something. To punch until his knuckles were bloody and bruised—a perfect match for his soul.

They had lost. After all the ridicule and torment from her brothers, he couldn't even deliver a stupid, fucking plastic trophy. It was the reason he'd shown up on this island in the first place. And if he couldn't do that, what made him think he could make the Boys and Girls Club a success?

It had been easy to agree to keep his fling with Penn under wraps. Whatever her reasons for keeping things a secret, he had his own. But the moment her father had accused him of being a bad influence, something had shifted. He'd realized he might want more than what they'd agreed to.

He had been hoping for a declaration, for some indication that she felt the same way. He was willing to support and defend her to the ends of the earth, but she still didn't trust him enough to have his back. To fight for him. To fight for herself.

Any hope of a future that might have sparked inside him had been extinguished.

So the moment his phone had beeped in his pocket, he knew he shouldn't have looked. But he had looked, and the image staring back at him was his worst nightmare. Someone had taken a picture of him and Penn dancing on stage. And it had gone viral. Jack had been the bearer of bad news and sent him the link to the *Toronto Gossip* site where speculation about a so-called relationship between them was the top story.

And wasn't that just the cherry on top of this disaster of a vacation.

Fuck!

He didn't need the media nosing around into his past. He didn't need anyone trying to make him into something he wasn't. He was no knight in shining armor. He wasn't going to sweep Penn off her feet and whisk her away to a happily ever after. This picture would only cause him grief at work and in his private life.

So he'd hit the gym. The only space in the world that gave him peace. Until he'd arrived here and realized that Penn had the same effect as the treadmill. She'd given him peace when he'd least expected it.

When he looked up, a movement in the mirror caught his attention.

He took his earbuds out but didn't stop running. "I can see you in the reflection, Penn."

"And here I thought I was being all stealth-ninja." She

walked into the gym slowly, carefully, as if walking across a bed of hot coals, with her concentration fixed on him.

She stopped at the back of the treadmill. Her frown was the heaviest he'd ever seen.

Losing the cup was just another on the list of bad things that had happened in his life. He feared that list was going to keep getting longer.

"You're upset." It wasn't a question.

"So what?" His broody emotions had always been the fuel to their love-hate relationship. The two of them were like oil and water. They just didn't mix, always in a constant battle for the upper hand.

"Talk to me, Cole," Penn pleaded.

The pain in her voice caused him to stumble on the machine. With a curse, he yanked the safety clip and jerked forward when the treadmill stopped abruptly. Panting heavily, he hung his head, both hands gripping the bars along the sides while he tried to catch his breath.

"Are you upset we didn't win the cup?"

He lifted his gaze, but not his head, and looked at her reflection in the mirror. Her shoulders were slumped forward, tears threatening to fall.

With a smile that didn't reach her eyes, she said, "There's always next year."

He laughed. He couldn't help it. Despite being utterly shattered inside, humor seemed to be the only emotion that didn't break him open in a chasm of hurt.

Did she think this only had to do with the cup?

He finally turned and faced her, and she backed up a few steps when their eyes met. He didn't mean to scare her. But in the end, that's all he'd end up doing. He was only capable of making her sad.

"There won't be a next year. Not for us. This was just…" He picked up the towel that hung across the bar and wiped it across his forehead. "We're coworkers. Friends. Nothing more." He hated the sound of his voice. Bitterness mixed with sadness and regret. His killer combination.

"What got you upset? What was in that text?"

"I'm not upset."

He wasn't going to lay it on the line for her, but he couldn't help the twinge of doubt, the one that told him he was no good, the one that confirmed he had no business trying to run a program that was supposed to help people.

"I'm pissed that I let you get me into the one situation I avoid like the plague."

"What…" She looked utterly confused. "What are you talking about?"

"What happened to your Google alerts?" He jerked his chin. "Check out *Toronto Gossip*. Looks like the entire world knows we crossed the coworker line."

She cursed under her breath, but they weren't as explicit as the ones that had gone through his head when he'd received the text.

She pulled out her phone, and he watched while she swiped her finger across the screen a few times. He brushed his brow with his towel, wiping away his anger, his frustration. His pathetic need to wrap her in his arms. He needed to do something to keep his hands occupied.

Somberly, she lowered her phone to her side. Her words were low and direct. "I'm sorry. I didn't think—"

"The publicity director for the Madewood Empire didn't think about it?" He scoffed. "I don't want this. I don't want people digging into my life. It's none of their business."

"I can spin this." She stepped forward, a determined set to her jaw. "I can make it like it never happened."

She was a little too eager to do that. It hurt. Despite wanting those pictures to disappear, he had liked the idea of her belonging to him. He just didn't want the entire world to know it.

"Besides, if there is a possibility that I'm going to be on the board, we can't…"

His head shot up.

"Sterling told me just before dinner. Did you know about it? About me being considered for the board?"

He shook his head. If he had known, he wouldn't have set foot in her hotel room. He wouldn't have acted on his impulses.

"I don't want anything from you, Cole. I didn't think that sleeping with you would get me…" She grabbed her hair at the roots and clenched her fists. "In fact, I owe you. You stayed here for me, to help me win."

He let out a low laugh. "A lot of good that did you." He couldn't even help her win a plastic trophy.

"It was the most selfless thing anyone has ever done for me."

It wasn't selfless. Not by a long shot.

A dozen emotions washed over her face. "Cole. I—"

"You don't owe me an explanation." He stepped off the treadmill, went to the bench, and picked up a weight. Resting his elbow on his knee, he pumped it up and down. "We both knew where this was going when we returned, board of directors or not."

He needed someone in his corner. He had thought that

person might be Penn, but she was just another woman that when push came to shove, wasn't willing to stand up and declare her choice. Him.

"If you're the reason my career progresses, my family will never take me seriously again. I'll never be their equal. Nothing I ever do will be worthwhile. They'll never see me the way I need them to if we're…"

She moved closer, but still not close enough to touch him. And fuck, he wanted her to touch him so badly. To pull him into an embrace and whisper that everything would be all right.

But he knew better. It was never going to be all right. Not for him.

"Do you understand?" She started to step forward but hesitated and sank back. "I'm sharing here, Cole. Things I've never shared with anyone."

He let out a long breath. "I'm honored that you let me into your bed but—"

"I'm not talking about spreading my legs, you jerk." Tears flooded her eyes. The sight of her crying, knowing that he'd caused that pain, ripped him apart. But if being a jerk helped her get over him, so be it.

"Penn, you don't want to go down this road." Looking back, the fact that his confession had been preempted that night in the hut was a sign. One that went off with warning bells and neon lights. He was never meant to tell her about his past. His story was repeating itself. He had dropped his guard, and it had blown up in his face.

"Yes, I do."

He looked up at her. She was holding herself back. He could tell by the way her feet were firmly planted on the floor, but her upper body was tilted forward, as if wanting to make contact. Or smack him upside the head.

"You opened up to me that night in the hut and walking on the beach," she said. "If we hadn't been interrupted, I'm pretty sure you would have told me more." She swiped at her cheeks. "And I want to know. All of it."

He placed the weight onto the floor and stood before brushing past her on his way to the door. It was a dick move. But he needed to touch her one last time before saying good-bye.

Her hand shot out and gripped his bicep. "Don't you dare walk out on me now. Talk to me! Please!" She was desperate. He heard it in her voice. It quivered and cracked as she spoke.

"No."

And then she did something, sank to a level he didn't think possible.

"Cole. I'm not your mother."

At that moment, his heart broke. Shattered into a million pieces. Not only because he couldn't have Penn, the only woman on earth who understood him, the only woman he might ever love, but because she had hit the nail right on the head. Without even having to tell her about his past, she had figured it out.

Was he really that transparent?

He regarded her warily. And although his heart was breaking, he felt nothing. Not anger. Not sadness. Not relief.

Nothing.

"Is that what you think of me?" he snarled. "That I'm a sad, sorry man with mommy issues?"

Exactly what you are.

She shook her head. "I just don't get you. Help me understand. We all have baggage." She let out a humorless laugh. "I just spent the last six days allowing you to witness mine firsthand."

He snorted. "You don't know anything about baggage."

She finally released his arm, but he didn't run away. Instead he faced her head on.

"You have no fucking idea how lucky you were." She took for granted every happy moment of her childhood. Her family might have flaws, but… "Normal is all I wanted my entire childhood. Normal. Stereotype. Belonging."

Hell, his entire life.

She gave him a long, questioning look, the gears turning in her head. "Is that what this is all about? You wanted to be a part of my family?"

"Christ." He swiped his hands over his face. "What the hell do you want from me?"

"I want the truth." She stomped her foot on the ground like a toddler. As if her tantrum was going to make him cave. "I want to know everything." She looked at him defiantly.

His words came out like a growl. "No, you don't. No one wants to know this kind of thing. My own damn mother didn't love me. Not enough to change. Not enough to keep me." He stepped closer, towering over her. "Is that what you wanted to hear, Penn?"

The desperation in her eyes faded away. She looked up at him with a mixture of fear and sorrow.

"Do you want to hear about how I had to steal in order to eat? That I had a mother who was too interested in fucking men for money that she forgot to buy groceries? That the reason I can't talk dirty is because I'd fall asleep to the sounds of disgusting men talking to my mother like a whore, saying those same things?" He laughed. "You know the funny thing about all that? She *was* a whore."

She stepped back. Pulled away from him, folding her arms across her abdomen as if keeping in the disgust.

Just as he'd suspected.

"It's not your fault," she whispered. "None of it."

"I know that," he barked. "But that doesn't change what happened." He kicked the weight hard, hoping it would make him hurt less inside, but even the sharp pain exploding in his foot didn't curb the ache in his soul.

Cole's body collapsed at the thought, and he sank down onto the bench, dropping his head in his hands. His throat tightened. Not because he was fighting to hold back tears. Not because the bile rising from his stomach threatened to spill out with one forceful heave.

Every molecule in his body told him not to look up at Penn. If he did, he'd never be able to look her in the eye again. Never be able to erase the memory of the horror that would surely be in her expression. But he did it anyway.

She was hanging on to one of the stationary bikes. Her shoulders were hunched forward, tears running down her cheeks. But she wasn't looking at him. She was staring at the floor. It wasn't horror etched on her beautiful face. It was shock and…devastation.

Their gazes met, and she opened her mouth to speak, but nothing came out.

"Oh, Cole," she whispered.

He saw it in her eyes. *Pity*. As clear as he'd seen her desire for him all week.

That was his picture-perfect childhood. His formative

years. Devoid of love and affection. Of healthy relationships. Of anything resembling normalcy.

Not until he was a teenager did Vivian find him and show him love. But that love also came with an expiration date. She had died much too young, much too early in his life. It had been a hard lesson, having the only love you've ever known ripped away from you.

And he wasn't making that mistake again.

"It's a lovely story, isn't it?" he mocked. "Poor Cole, taken away from his own mother after too many years of neglect. Poor Cole, even his own mother didn't love him enough to straighten up. How can I expect *anyone* to love me, to put me first, when my own mother couldn't even do it?"

He stood defiantly, shielding himself behind the impenetrable wall he kept between him and the rest of the world. Penn had chipped away at it all week, and if he had been any weaker, he might have let her kick it down completely. But what purpose would that serve? Without the barrier, he was a black hole of darkness, capable of pulling everyone into the chaos with him.

So he steeled his emotions. Slammed them down, once again, under lock and key. Never to be toyed with again.

Finally, Penn spoke. "Vivian Madewood loved you. Like you were her own child."

He nodded sadly. "And I loved Vivian. I loved everything about her. She was caring, humble, and most of all, forgiving. She forgave me every time I lashed out and made her feel like shit." He look into Penn's eyes. "Kind of like with you, Penn. Don't you see? That's all I know how to do—lash out and reject, make others feel worthless. Because that's all I am."

More tears streamed down Penn's face. "You're the furthest thing from worthless, Cole. Please…" She whispered his name over and over, shaking her head.

It killed him. Her pain. He knew with every breath she ached for him. He wanted to reach out and wrap his arms around her, feel her embrace him, and surround him with her love and her goodness. More than anything he wanted to hear her whisper that he meant something, anything, to her, and that everything would be all right.

But he kept his hands at his sides. Because even if she might care, she didn't care enough to change anything. Even Penn couldn't fix him.

And he loved her too much to put her through the inevitable.

It was true. Everything he'd done for her this week was because he loved her. He knew that now. She probably deserved to know that he loved her. But more than that, she deserved to know there was no future between them.

"It's best if we just go back to the way things were before we came here." He took a deep breath. "We're coworkers. Friends, I guess. That's it."

She choked out a sob. "Please," she cried, reaching for him, but he pulled away.

He had to be strong.

"You don't want to be promoted because you're sleeping around the company, and I don't want my personal life, past or present, splashed around the tabloids."

Reporters were ruthless. Cunning. They'd posted a sex tape of his brother online, for fuck's sake. He couldn't risk the world finding out how he'd grown up, speculating and reading into his relationships to see if his past carried into his present. He loved her, but right now, the thought of his past being public knowledge scared him more than the thought of losing her.

She collapsed against the bike, wrapping her arms around herself.

He had to walk past her on his way to the door. When his arm brushed hers, he lowered his head and whispered, "When you go back to your room and look in the mirror, remember who it was that crushed your beautiful spirit. Remember *that* the next time you think you and I would ever be a good idea."

With a heavy breath, and an ache in his heart too profound for words, he walked away. Just as the memories of his past haunted him, he'd carry the heartbreaking sound of her sobbing with him for the rest of his life.

Chapter Fifteen

Penn stared at the empty closet in Cole's hotel room. She'd convinced a maid to let her in, pretending there was an emergency.

But there was no emergency. Just the sick, heavy lump of regret that had settled in her stomach.

She'd needed some time to collect her thoughts after he'd laid the truth at her feet. Apparently, it was just enough time for him to pack his bags and leave without a good-bye.

His past had been worse than she'd ever imagined. As long as she lived, she'd never forget the sight of him standing in that gym. For such a solid man, broad shoulders and tall frame, he had shrunk into himself. It was the moment he walked out on her that she realized she loved him. Or it was the moment she was brave enough to accept it, because she'd probably always loved him.

But how he grew up and where he came from didn't matter to her. She knew he had a dark side. She knew he'd had a difficult childhood, and she had loved him anyway. For the boy he'd been. For the man he'd become.

They had finally crossed that invisible line. The one where he lowered his defensive walls and let her in. But as soon as he'd told her everything, he'd built them right back up, stronger and thicker than ever.

Now he was gone.

And it was all her fault.

She couldn't live like this anymore, letting her fears control her. She raced out of his room toward the elevator and down through the lobby to find her family.

She'd let her fear of their disapproval control her, to the point that she wasn't brave enough to stand up for Cole when he needed it. Maybe if she had fought for him, if she had told him how she felt, he would have had a reason to stay. But she'd stayed silent and let him suffer her father's accusations. He'd spent the entire week trying to get her to open up to her family because he believed in her, supported her, flaws and all. And she'd betrayed him by not returning that favor.

She should be sad. She should be crying in the corner like a little girl because her heart was broken. Instead, she was angry.

Blood-boiling angry. At herself.

And there were a few people she needed to set straight.

She walked with determination through the hotel complex toward the beach. The waves, the wildlife, and the chatter of the other guests had all morphed into a buzzing noise that echoed in her ears.

She stopped at the edge of the sand. Just in front of her, her family was having a great time celebrating their version of a closing ceremony with a bonfire, but she had nothing to celebrate. She had lost more than just a trophy. She had lost the man she loved.

If she hadn't been so angry, she would have admired that the hotel staff had dug out a pit in the sand and formed a seating area around the small fire with soft cushions and pillows. They'd even set up a table with all of the fixings for s'mores.

"Penn, there you are," Christine said, while putting her roasted marshmallow on top of chocolate and graham cracker. "We've…" Christine's face fell when she looked up at her. "What's wrong?"

So she had her angry face on. Good.

Andy ran up from out of nowhere and yanked on Penn's arm. "Aunt Pennie, will you build a sand castle with me?"

She looked down at her nephew, excitement and innocence in his eyes. Immediately, she thought of Cole. Of what his life must have been like at Andy's age. Going hungry. Having to endure strange men coming into the one place that was supposed to be safe. Her chest tightened, and she wiped away a tear that fell from her cheek.

She pulled Andy closer into a tight hug. "In a little while. I have to talk to the adults first."

When she approached the bonfire, her parents and siblings were engaged in conversation and barely noticed her arrival.

Until Dave snickered. "Where's Celebrity Chef?"

Her hands fisted at her sides. "He had to go home."

"Kitchen emergency?" Dave slapped his knee in amusement.

"They probably had to serve frozen chicken instead of

fresh," Ian said, getting in on the Cole bashing.

Penn looked over at Pete, trying to ground herself.

Keep your cool, Penn.

"Madewood restaurants serve sub-par food." Beth joined in, too. "News at eleven."

Penn crossed her arms over her chest. "You really shouldn't trash talk someone who's not here to defend themselves."

"What's Celebrity Chef going to do?" Dave held out his arms as if welcoming a confrontation. "Force feed me cheesecake until I puke?"

She tried to take her brother's joking in stride, but all she saw was red.

"No, you douche," she spat out the words. They rolled off her tongue so easily.

Damn that felt good.

"I will." She eyed her family, one by one, taking a deep breath before saying, "Because I love him."

"I knew it!" Beth yelled out, jumping from her seat.

With the exception of her, the rest of the family was silent.

"I love him." The more she said it out loud, the more her heart tightened because she knew it was a lost cause.

She stepped forward, wanting to make sure the next words out of her mouth were heard loud and clear, but the flames were damn hot. She settled for moving to the outer edge of the pit, opposite Beth.

"I shouldn't have lied about us. Although, we weren't really an us, still aren't an us, but I don't want to lie anymore. Not about Cole. Not about who I am. Never again."

"I don't like this one bit, Pennie," her father said. "That boy—"

"That boy is kind," she interrupted. "Ambitious. Selfless

and supportive. He likes me just the way I am, which is a hell of a lot more than I can say for you."

She'd thought she'd made some progress with her siblings the other night at the club. She'd thought she'd given them enough to realize on their own that she wasn't the little girl they thought she was. But it hadn't been welcomed.

These were the people who were supposed to love her no matter what. And it was damn time they started.

"If you love each other so much," Dave retaliated. "Why did he leave you, Pennie?"

At the sound of her nickname, something snapped. All of the anger she'd been holding back exploded.

"For the last time, my name is not Pennie!" She spit out the nickname with as much contempt as she could muster.

Dave jerked back at her outburst. A gasp sounded on the opposite side of the bonfire. She didn't blame them; she barely recognized her own voice.

"It's Penn or Pennelope."

She wanted to believe it was the use of her nickname that had sparked her outrage, but if she was honest, Dave's comment had hit too close to home. She did love Cole, and he'd left her.

Her failure to stand up and fight for him had forced him to relive his traumatic past. How was she ever going to get him to trust her, love her, after that? She only hoped that when she returned home, they might be able to salvage some kind of a friendship.

"Look at me. I am not the chubby, nerdy, uncoordinated wallflower I was when I was fifteen years old. I have a tattoo. I own fifty-six pairs of stilettos that probably cost as much as a year's college tuition. I dance on tables. *I'm* the bad influence." She looked over at her father, trying to prove a point. Her behavior had nothing to do with Cole.

She glowered at them. Maybe just at Dave and Beth.

"And I like to say fuck." She held her arms out and let her head fall back. "Fuck. Fuck. Fuck. Fuck."

"Aunt Pennie said a bad word," Andy yelled out.

"Yes, Andy. I did." She turned to look at the little ones who were off by themselves away from the fire. "And one day, you will, too."

"Penn, really." Ian thrust up his arm and let it fall down to his knee with a thump. "Do you have to encourage my child to swear?"

"I'm just telling it like it is."

Other than Pete and Christine, the rest of her family stared at her in shock. Dave's mouth was practically on the sand. Her father's jaw twitched. He was holding in his anger. She could see it clearly even through the dancing flames. She couldn't decipher the look on her mother's face.

"That was five F-bombs," Dave yelled, then turned to her father. "So fifty pushups, right, Dad?" His current expression was the same one she'd seen on her brother for her entire life. The look of a man seeking approval.

"Tell me something, Dave." She crossed her arms over her chest. "Does it make you happy doing everything Dad tells you to do? He wanted you to be a teacher, so you did. He wanted you to play football. So you did. He wanted you to get married and have a family. And you did." She held out her hand, gesturing to Beth, who now paced the edge of the pit with Hannah in her arms.

"You think that just because I didn't follow the path Dad wanted me to that I'm unsuccessful. You tease me. You dismiss me and my work." She choked back tears. "I'll have you know Cole and his brothers help thousands of kids a year, Dad. In different ways than you do, but they're changing lives just like you are. All of my work, everything I do, supports their efforts. So I *am* helping kids. I *am* making a difference. But I'm doing it my own way. Not yours." She took a deep breath. "I don't want to be a drone. A damn carbon copy of the rest of you."

When this was all over, she was going to have to apologize to Pete and Christine. She didn't have the same harsh feelings about them as she did the rest of her family, even though Pete had toed the Foster line his entire life.

She just hadn't been able to swallow the identity pill that would make her exactly like the rest of them. She wanted to do something completely different. Achieve it all on her own. On her own merit and determination. Which was why her job with the Madewood family was so important. Which was why, if she got a spot on the board, she didn't want it to be tainted because people found out she'd had a sexual relationship with Cole.

"Are you quite finished making a scene?" Her father looked behind him. Probably making sure that no one was paying attention to her inappropriate outburst. But the only people on the beach were a few couples who were too engrossed in each other to care about her freak out.

She narrowed her eyes, thinking about it, staring at the blank faces of most of her siblings. She'd said her piece. She'd tried. The ball was now in their corner.

With a heavy breath, she grabbed one of the s'mores sticks and began poking the fire. "Yes, thank you."

"What I don't understand is where this is all coming

from," her mother said, shooting a disapproving look at her father. Interesting.

"It was the only way to make you actually listen."

Which was true, but it had everything to do with being angry that she'd fucked up with Cole. His departure was the straw that broke the camel's back, forcing her to be true to herself.

"You all know nothing about me. Yes, it's my own fault. I should have told you I was changing. But I didn't dare, because I was afraid of being criticized or laughed at, and—" She'd hidden herself from her family out of fear. "I was afraid that you wouldn't love me anymore."

"That's preposterous," her father scoffed.

"Not entirely, dear," her mother responded.

The stick Penn was holding caught on fire when she froze at her mother's words.

"What are you saying?" Her father had a furious look on his face.

Penn shoved the stick into the sand, putting out the flame, and quickly returned to the scene between her parents.

"You made it very clear that if any one of our children didn't excel at sports or follow in your footsteps, they weren't good enough. You showered our sons with love and affection because they could throw a ball through a hoop. But Pennelope? Not so much."

Penn still couldn't shoot a free throw to save her life. And the surfing fiasco the other day had proven her aversion to water sports was warranted.

"I—" Her father gaped. "That's not—"

"Forty years. We've been married for forty years, and I have always stood by you. But I've always thought you pushed the children too hard."

Penn looked over at Pete. His face was frozen in shock.

Her mother sighed. "They all seemed to like competition. Thrived on it. So I never questioned your methods. But apparently that wasn't really the case." She turned to Penn. "I thought you were happy, Pennelope. If I'd known you weren't, I would have spoken up years ago."

She stared blankly at her mother. She appreciated the support, if belated, but right now, there were too many thoughts spinning around in her head. The only words she could muster were, "Thanks, Mom."

Penn felt lighter than she had all week. She felt like herself. And she owed it all to Cole.

She wasn't going to feel bad anymore about not following the same family drum. She had so many other qualities that not living up to the few skills her father valued would no longer define her as a person. Not as a daughter, or a sister, or a friend. Or as a woman.

"I think the other kids and I should go for a walk down the beach." Her mother patted her father's knee and stood, shuffling the rest of her siblings out of the pit toward the shoreline.

Then it was just her and her father.

"Pennelope?" Her father's voice carried over the sizzle and crackle of the fire.

But she said nothing.

The next thing she knew, he loomed over her with his hands on his hips. The classic Harold Foster I-mean-business stance.

When she still didn't acknowledge him, he sank down into the sand beside her, letting out a tiny groan on his way down.

Silence fell between them as she once again poked the stick into the ash, but her father broke it with a sigh. "I'll admit it. I did want you to be like your brothers."

Finally. The truth. She only hoped it would set her free.

"I couldn't relate to you. I didn't know how to interact with a little girl. So I treated you like a boy. In hindsight, maybe that wasn't the best idea."

"You wanted me to be a demure little girl who said yes, please, and thank you, but also a warrior on the field. It was impossible to live up to."

So, she had stopped trying. Maybe if she had rebelled against it all as a teenager, her entire life might have played out differently.

"But you are my little girl." He lifted her chin and wiped away a tear she hadn't even known was there. "And my little girl isn't supposed to swear or wear skimpy clothing."

"But don't you get it? The pressure to be a good girl meant I never had any fun. So, when I went off to college, boy, did I have fun."

Frat parties. Beer bongs. Dating. Lots and lots of dating.

He held up his hands. "I don't want to know."

She had no intention of giving him details. There were some things a girl needed to keep to herself.

Her father shook his head, confusion again washing over his face. "I want the world for you, Pennelope, but I just don't understand you."

"You don't have to, Dad." Waves crashed loudly in the distance, startling her. "It's not your—"

Her father grabbed her chin, forcing her to look over at him. "What if I want to understand?"

She smiled. She had to give him credit. He was trying. Trying to relate to her on a level he wasn't familiar with—an emotional level. Harold Foster wasn't the most demonstrative man in the world.

"I push you because I want you to succeed."

"I have succeeded." She straightened, her body going into defense mode. "I've tried so hard to make you proud, Dad, but you make it impossible when you refuse to see things outside your comfort zone."

"I do like my comfort zone." He laughed softly. "I just want you to have the same wonderful life that I've had with your mother, with you kids."

Crap. Now he was making her feel guilty for poo-pooing his very normal, mundane life. It made him happy.

She leaned against him and rested her head on his shoulder. She didn't remember ever doing this as a kid. And for the first time ever, she felt a tiny bond with her father. One that wasn't built on sports or false personas. For the first time, he was truly seeing her, and she saw the love in his eyes as he looked at her.

She might not have achieved what she'd set out to do. She hadn't won the cup. But this trip hadn't all been for nothing. Not even close.

She'd finally been able to get everything off her chest with her family. From now on, she would be herself, good-girl persona not required.

"I have to admit, as much as I disliked you being so... different, I hadn't seen you that happy in a long time."

She wasn't so happy anymore.

"Thanks to Cole," she said.

"So you love him."

She shrugged— A gesture that immediately made her think of him.

She probably couldn't do a lot of things now, without thinking of him.

"Why did he leave?" he asked. "Is it because you didn't win the cup?"

She wished that were true. Then she wouldn't have died a little inside hearing the awful details of his past. She wouldn't have had to watch him walk away. That was something she might never recover from.

She shook her head, willing away the tears threatening to fall. She didn't want to cry in front of her father. She was already too vulnerable right now. "Because I didn't give him a reason to stay."

When push came to shove, she couldn't be what he'd needed. She'd let her fears push him away. And she might never get him back.

She had walked into this situation with her eyes wide open. She'd known the end game might very well strain their relationship, but she had no idea that it would break her heart.

"It's just not meant to be, Dad. Regardless of what I want."

Her father pulled away, straightening his shoulders, looking down at her with conviction. "If there's one thing I taught you, young lady, it's never to give up. To fight for what you want."

Too bad she'd forgotten that when it mattered most.

"If this boy makes you happy, if he's what you want, then you fight for him." He hugged her into his side. "If you love someone, don't be a schmuck like me. Say it. Prove it. Life is too short to waste assuming the world is right, when it's so very wrong."

The more time she'd spent with Cole, the harder it became to keep her emotions out of the game. She'd spent her entire life being smart. Made every decision with her head, not her heart or libido. But Cole Murphy scrambled her brain, leaving it useless and ineffective.

No matter how much she might have wanted this week in paradise to change the game between them, it had backfired. He had finally trusted her enough to break down the steel and cement he'd erected around his heart. And she'd been the one who'd forced him to put it back up.

"Thanks, Dad."

He kissed her forehead and got up. "Are you going to be all right?"

She would be. Eventually.

Cole wasn't ready. For her. For a life filled with love. He might never be ready.

She knew nothing in his history could be bad enough to scare her away. Even the parts she didn't know yet. But even if her gut told her she was willing to fight for him, for his past, for their future, she couldn't do that with a man who wouldn't let her in.

Chapter Sixteen

As soon as the plane touched down, Cole ran full speed ahead with the club, working directly with their investors and volunteers. A job he usually reserved for Penn. Never in a million years would he have thought he'd become the social butterfly in the family. But something had changed in him. And he knew it had everything to do with her.

Penn.

He loved her. With every fiber of his being. And he'd left her in Hawaii. Left without a word, without a good-bye. He just hadn't known how to give his heart away. He still didn't. For so long, he'd held it tight, kept it locked up, offering his love to only two women in his life — his biological mother, who'd broken it with her skewed priorities, and Vivian, who had held it so sacred, but had left this world so quickly she'd taken a piece of it with her.

For so long he'd walked around with a dark cloud, unable to shake it. It seeped into his being, into his very soul.

But it was Penn that brought him peace. She tuned out the world around him and brought everything into perspective. Because she was so daring, carefree, and light. The exact opposite of his moody brooding. She made him lighter simply by being near him.

Although he'd made a good effort to keep his darkness in check in Hawaii, the moment things got tough, he'd floundered and lost his way. He'd let it take over. Because that's how it would always be.

How could he possibly subject Penn to that kind of future?

Walking away had made it easier on both of them. She didn't have to choose, and he didn't have to find out what that choice might be.

Like a coward, he steered clear of his restaurant this morning, knowing Penn would be back to work. She knew his deepest, darkest, most haunting secrets, and he just wasn't ready to face her yet.

He walked through the back door of Carmel, hoping to find Finn. Instead, he found Veronica, sitting behind Finn's desk.

"Hey, Cole. What brings you by?" She winced and unconsciously rubbed her ample baby belly.

"I...uh...was looking for Finn."

She stopped what she was doing and set the papers down in front of her. "He's in Niagara."

Shit. Cole had been there when Finn booked his hotel room. He should have just told the truth.

"He's tasting new—" Her soft half-sigh, half-moan carried from the desk. "Oh!" Suddenly, Veronica stood and grabbed her belly, doubling over in pain.

"V?" Terror instantly gripped him, and everything else

was forgotten. She didn't look so good. All of the color had drained from her face. She sounded even worse. "Are you all right?"

"I don't know." She used the desk as a crutch and walked toward him. When she came around the desk corner, he gasped. She had blood all over her pants.

No, no, this was not happening. He broke into a sweat.

"V, stay calm but… You're bleeding."

"Wha—*What*?"

She tried to look down, but her stomach was in the way, so she touched the juncture of her thighs and cried out when she pulled her hand away covered in blood. "Cole! Oh my God!"

He raced over and pulled her into a hug, then cradled her against his side as he headed for the door. "Come on, we're going to the hospital."

"Finn?" She looked up at him, her face wrenched in pain and a tear trickling down her cheek.

"I'll call him on the way. Let's just get you there."

On the way out, he grabbed some tablecloths from the storage room and spread them over the passenger seat of his car. When she was settled, he buckled her in, then sprinted around to the driver's seat. Hopping in, he pulled out his phone and hit speed dial.

Finn answered on the third ring. "Hel—"

"Brother, you better get your ass back here, this instant." The engine roared to life.

"What's wrong?" Finn demanded.

"I'm taking V to the hospital. There's blood—"

"*What?*"

Cole's heart thundered. He swallowed hard and took

a corner on two wheels. "She's in pain, and dude, I— I'm taking her to the hospital as fast as I can."

Silence.

Veronica gripped his arm. "Finn!" she cried out, gasping at another pain.

"I'm leaving right now," his brother yelled. "Just…tell her to hold it until I get there."

"Hold what? Not like she can h—"

Veronica screamed, clutching the bottom of her belly with one hand and Cole's arm with the other.

"Gotta go, Brother." He tossed the phone on the console and drove like a demon.

They were taken into the emergency room immediately. He'd been pushed out of the way by nurses and banished to the corner of the makeshift room walled by a blue curtain. Every sight and sound was magnified—the insistent beep of the machines, the sound of the automatic doors behind them, the squeeze of gel out of a bottle. In his corner, he took the time to call Neil and Jack, informing them of the situation. He sent a text to Finn, giving him an update.

So far, it had been a nightmare. But he'd stayed with Veronica the whole time, taking Finn's place until he arrived. V was in so much pain she looked like a ghost of her normal self. Her hair was soaked with sweat. Her face red and splotchy. And every once in a while, a tear would stream down her cheek, despite Cole's murmurs of reassurance that everything would be all right.

Was he a total asshat for silently thanking God for giving him a penis?

When they told her she had a placental abruption and was going to need a C-section, she looked up at him with tears in her eyes, terror scattering across her face. "I'm scared."

He wished he could take her pain away. He wished he could change the circumstances.

Where the fuck was Finn?

Cole was freaking out more and more by the minute. He actually felt faint.

He took her hand. "It'll be fine, V. Should I maybe go get Sterling or—"

She clamped down on his hand. "Don't go. Please, Cole."

He sucked in a calming breath.

Man up, Murphy.

He heard Penn's voice in his head. It was exactly something she'd say to him when she was calling him out.

"Of course I won't." He patted Veronica's hand, and she relaxed her grip a little. "And Finn will be here soon." He pulled a chair closer to the bed and clasped her hand in his.

And they waited.

Finally, Finn raced through the door. "Where is she? What's happening?"

Fear was plastered all over his face, but that turned to relief when he spotted Veronica on the bed. New tears crested in her eyes when she saw him. He hurried over to her. Planting a soft kiss on her lips, he wiped away her tears and murmured into her ear.

Cole's heart suddenly hurt. Seeing them together on the verge of this life-changing event made him feel all alone.

He quietly headed for the door.

A hand gripped his shoulder and he turned. Fear darkened his brother's eyes, and it tore him apart. "Thanks, man. For taking care of her."

Cole pulled him into a heartfelt hug, offering all of his strength and courage. "It's going to be okay, bro. I promise."

He headed out to the waiting room, stopping outside the door to look at his worried family huddled in the semi-circle of green plastic chairs. He didn't know what he would do if anything happened to a single one of them. They all meant the world to him.

Sterling's eyes were rimmed red, and in an intimate gesture, Jack swiped away a stray tear from her cheek, then pulled her close. Neil and Carson were both stoic; neither of them expressed their feelings outwardly. But by the way Neil fisted one hand at his side, he knew he had a war waging inside of him. Mark and Cal, Veronica's brothers, sat together on the far right. Cal banged the back of his head against the wall in a steady rhythm, while Mark hid his face in his hands as he rested his elbows on his knees. He turned his attention to the left, and there was Penn. She sat by herself, aimlessly scrolling through her phone.

His heart pounded inside his chest like a sledgehammer. No matter how much distance he gave himself, his reaction to her was always the same. A visceral need to touch her, claim her for himself.

"Cole!" Sterling spotted him just as he opened the door, and the whole family jumped up and rushed forward.

"Is she okay?" Cal asked.

Cole ran his hand through his hair and told them everything he knew. Afterward, although he hadn't done much to ease their worry, they all settled down to wait.

But Cole was restless and paced the room. He couldn't stop the feeling of dread from settling in his stomach. The "what ifs" bombarded his brain. There were too many possible outcomes for him to even keep a level head. *This* feeling was exactly why he distanced himself. Even with the people he loved most in the world, he just couldn't bring himself to let them in. He couldn't risk the utter devastation when the inevitable loss happened.

Another forty minutes passed. It was taking too long. Something was wrong.

"Are you doing all right?" He tensed when he felt Penn's hand slide up his back to his shoulder and squeeze.

He hadn't been doing all right. He had been panicked. Restless. Worried. Useless. There was no end to the flurry of emotions that had rushed through his system over the last couple hours. But right now, with Penn's bright eyes and warm body, the world could blow up around him, and he'd be calm—completely at ease because she was near.

To ease her worry, he turned and smiled, although it wasn't his brightest.

"Veronica is going to be fine." She grabbed his hand. "She's tough, and so is that baby." He saw it there in her eyes, the worry for not only Veronica and the baby, but for him.

He nodded.

"I know it's hard for you to see me." She dipped her head, lowering her gaze to the floor. "It's hard for me, too."

Instinctively, he reached out and placed his index finger under her chin, then raised her head to meet his gaze. Penn shouldn't look down. Not for anyone.

"We're still friends." It was impossible for him not to remember how her lips felt against his when she blurted, "I'm here if you need to talk." Her eyes watered, tears pooling at the sides. "And you have to know that nothing's changed the way I—"

"She's beautiful!" Finn burst through the doors of the waiting room. His eyes were shiny with happy tears, his lips curved up in the biggest smile Cole had ever seen. "Just like her mother."

Cole let out a steady breath, relief and happiness washing over him. They were all right. Both of them.

He turned to Penn who was smiling widely, unable to get her half-admission out of his head.

The way what?

Did she have the same feelings he did? Or was she trying to tell him she still wanted to keep her distance because of her career?

He searched her face for an answer, but she gave away nothing. With one last squeeze to his forearm, Penn left him standing in the corner and joined the group, bombarding Finn with questions and congratulations.

The C-section had been touch and go, but mom and baby were doing just fine.

A flurry of emotions washed over Cole like a wave. First relief. Then happiness. A strange feeling he was somehow getting used to.

Cole had bullied his way to the front of the line to see Veronica and the baby, using the fact that he'd brought Veronica to the hospital as ammunition.

He sprinted, along with Sterling, to the private room she'd been placed in. The baby was close enough to full term that she didn't need to be put into an incubator. Although the delivery had been wrought with complications, the result was a perfectly healthy, seven-pound, eight-ounce little girl.

Sterling pushed ahead of him, squealing as she raced over

to the bed. She immediately began cooing and mumbling indecipherable words.

When he walked in, Finn stood by the window, a wide smile on his face. He'd never seen his brother so proud. Veronica practically glowed, the complete opposite of what she'd looked like prior to delivery. It was like that tiny baby she held in her arms had given *her* new life.

He took his time approaching the bed, cautiously making his way. Unsure of what to do. What to say.

"Uncle Cole." Veronica beamed up at him. "Come and meet your niece, Vivian."

He stopped in his tracks, choking down a hard swallow.

Vivian. They couldn't have picked a better name.

Sterling went back to squealing now that she knew the baby's name.

When he reached the bed and peeked inside the pink blanket, all of his hesitation slipped away.

She was so tiny. So fidgety. So completely beautiful.

"This is a *private* room," Neil's voice boomed from the other side of the door. "We should be able to have as many visitors as we want."

Carson walked in, shaking her head with a smile. Mark and Cal rushed into the room. Mark immediately embraced Veronica, kissing her on the forehead, relief taking over his face.

All of them turned when Neil walked into the room. He simply shrugged. "Like we're going to play by the rules."

Jack clapped him on the back, then closed the door.

Penn was nowhere to be seen.

He pushed aside his disappointment and embraced the feeling in the room. It was a buzz with high-pitched voices and soft sighs. With happiness. Excitement.

Cole gazed at the faces of his family. His unconventional family. Four men brought together by the kindness of one woman. There were no blood relationships. No childhood memories made together. But these people had brought him more happiness than he'd ever known.

He had romanticized the idea of a normal family. In Hawaii, he'd thought the Foster family symbolized just that — happy people sharing a perfect bond. But they were just as flawed and chaotic as anyone.

He'd been totally disillusioned.

Family wasn't about blood. Or challenges. Or rivalries. Family was about the people who loved you no matter what. The circle of people who supported you.

And he had that, right here.

But there was one person missing, the most important person. He'd given up on her too quickly. Instead of accepting her, he'd pushed her away. He'd thought that would keep his heart from breaking.

But he'd been sorely mistaken.

To say he fucked up with her was the understatement of the century.

A warm hand clapped onto his shoulder. "I'm glad you were there for Veronica." Finn squeezed his hand. "I'm glad you're here for me."

He turned to his brother, taking in the goofy smile he'd had since they were kids, then looked over at Veronica and the baby. At that moment, something inside him broke.

Despite the horrible ending to the trip, since Hawaii, Cole had never felt so settled. So content with himself. So... whole. He had battled his demons, that broken, humiliated little boy, and for the first time he'd won.

Telling Penn had been the difference. His family was supposed to love him no matter what had happened when he was a child. But Penn, she had just told him she'd be there for him despite his past.

It would always be there; it wouldn't be healthy to pretend otherwise. But he was worth far more than what he'd believed. His past wasn't his future.

It was Penn who had enabled him to see a different kind of life. And the arrival of that perfect, little baby made him want to start over.

With new life, he would bury his past.

And there was only one thing he wanted or needed in his future.

Penn.

She was the only person that fit the other half of his broken heart.

He needed to get down on his knees and beg her forgiveness. Tomorrow was registration day for the very first fall session of the Madewood Boys and Girls Club. And he knew exactly what he had to do.

Chapter Seventeen

Penn watched from her perch behind the bar with a smile, smoothing down the front of her black, satin dress.

There were at least a hundred parents and children waiting outside Bistro to sign up for the Madewood Boys and Girls Club. The line was out the door and around the block. To say her efforts in promoting the sign-up were successful was the understatement of the year.

The whole Madewood family was present today, each with a special job to do tending to parents and kids and making sure the refreshments were refilled. Cole stood at the front door, greeting the parents and children, and at one point, their gazes locked. He mouthed the words "Thank you," and her heart swelled.

All of her work and stress about making this day a success had been worth it. With one look, he'd made it all matter. Funny how she'd been searching for that approval her entire life, something her family could never give, and with one simple look, Cole had given her everything she needed.

She loved him. Wanted him more than her next breath. But he was distant. She knew it had everything to do with her knowing his secrets. She'd done her best to put him at ease yesterday, but with all the commotion, it wasn't the best time.

A few hours into the day and Penn snuck off into the kitchen to catch her breath. She rested her palms on the large island in the middle of the room and took a deep breath. It smelled like garlic and mint.

She jumped when Cole's smooth voice carried over her shoulder.

"This turnout is incredible." A tingle raced up her spine. Too many memories. Too many hot nights with that tone, that stern whisper in her ear. She'd never be able to erase those memories.

You don't want to.

He was only a few steps away when she turned to face him, and his smoldering stare ignited her entire body. He'd set every molecule on fire with the way his eyes roamed over her, then finally settled on her lips. He licked his, like he wanted to kiss her. Like he wanted to take her into his office and ravage her just like he had in Hawaii.

He wasn't playing fair. He couldn't keep changing his feelings whenever the mood struck, because her heart would break every time he distanced himself again.

He reached forward and grabbed her hand in his. "Truly. Thank you."

She blew out a nervous breath and didn't miss the small smile that curved at the side of his lips at her discomfort.

Damn him. Damn. It. All.

Instead of giving him the satisfaction, she resorted to their old pattern of communicating. "What can I say, I'm good at my job."

Sarcastic banter. That should do the trick.

Right. Because that never added any fuel to the fire of lust burning between your legs.

When she noticed movement behind Cole, she peeked around him and gasped when she found her entire family huddled together in the kitchen doorway.

"I invited some guests today," he said, turning to face them. "I thought they'd appreciate your hard work."

Her parents wore proud smiles. Her brothers and sisters-in-law were also there. Pete and Christine had been to Bistro dozens of times over the years but never in the kitchen. They looked around in wonder. Dave and Beth looked uncomfortable, which was uncharacteristic for the boisterous couple. Ian held Cathy tightly around the waist who stared in awe as the rest of Cole's family joined them. This was a dream come true for her—all four Madewood boys in one spot.

She smiled at her best friend. Sterling, whose hand was entwined with Jack's. Finn was there, without Veronica, who was still recovering from giving birth. Which made his appearance even more special.

"Penn's family," Neil boomed in that get-everyone's-attention tone. He had his hand clamped around Carson's waist, holding so tightly it was as if she was his lifeline. "Perfect timing."

Perfect…what?

"Wha… What are you guys doing here?"

"Cole invited us," her father said. "He wanted us to see

what you did." He looked shocked. "You did all that?" He pointed out to the restaurant.

They all looked shocked. Well fu—

"Of course she did," Cole responded for her.

"I helped." She couldn't take all the credit. This was Cole's idea. She'd just made the idea a reality.

"I couldn't have done it without you." His words were warm and heartfelt in her ear.

Not. Playing. Fair.

Wait, why was he standing so close?

What the hell was going on? She was always in the loop. She *was* the damn loop.

"As you may know," Neil addressed the crowd. "Our friend, Gloria York, has stepped down from the board of directors of the Vivian Madewood Foundation."

Oh, God. Was this it? Were they actually going to tell her she was being considered for the job? Maybe it would finally prove to her family that she did more than just answer the phones for celebrities.

"My brothers and I thought long and hard about who we wanted to take her place." Finn elbowed Neil in the ribs. "All right." He held up his hand in defense. "We didn't have to think very long or hard because the answer was a no-brainer." He smiled and made an effort to meet the eyes of every member of her family. "There is only one woman we want for this job. Someone who already knows how we think, what we like, and can diffuse our arguments, because essentially, she'd be the tiebreaker."

He turned and stared directly at her. "A woman who constantly one-ups herself with every project because she is the most dedicated, resourceful, and hard-working woman

I've ever met." Her breath caught in her throat when her name escaped his lips. "Penn, we'd love for you to join the board."

Excitement swelled in her chest. She looked over at Cole who gave her a small smile. He'd stayed hidden in the shadows, allowing Neil to be the one to make the announcement. Knowing how much it meant that he not be the reason she got the job.

"Pennie!" Her mother squealed, then held up her finger and waited a beat before correcting herself. "Pennelope. Congratulations."

Pete immediately walked over and put his arm around her shoulders. He leaned in and whispered into her ear, "I know how much you wanted this." In a louder voice, he said, "Congratulations."

Neil pulled out an envelope and handed it over. "The papers are in order. All you have to do is sign."

She opened her mouth to speak, but nothing came out. "You..." How could they have done this so fast? "You couldn't have gotten these done in a day."

"You can get a lot done when you throw money at something," Neil said. "Besides, Cole was the one who wanted us to make the announcement today."

She looked over at him. He had a sly smile curving at the side of his lips. He had something up his sleeve. He was never this gleeful. Never.

"So what's your answer, Penn?" Jack winked as he rubbed his hand up and down Sterling's bicep. That tiny, intimate gesture made her feel lonely. But she shook it off. This was her moment. And she wasn't going to let regret over her feelings for Cole ruin it.

"I say…yes! Of course."

She ran up to Finn and gave him a huge hug. Then she did the same with Jack and Neil. Of course, Neil took the opportunity to lift her up, leaving her legs to dangle like a rag doll.

So far the day had been a success, and this was just the cherry on top. And she needed all the happiness she could get.

"Now that the board nomination has been made…" Cole yelled from behind. She whirled around and faced him. When their gazes met, he continued, "I'd like to formally resign from my position on the board." He handed Neil a white envelope.

"What the fuck is this?" Neil glared at him. "I'm not accepting this."

"You're going to have to." He turned his attention to Penn. "Even though there may not be a formal rule about board members dating, I want there to be no question that Penn has earned every bit of this herself."

After a moment of hesitation, everyone's eyes turned to Penn. Nervousness crawled up her neck and set her cheeks on fire.

"I want to set the record straight," Cole continued. "You earned your spot on the board without any help from me, but let's remind everyone exactly what we've gotten ourselves into."

My family is here, Murphy. If you so much as—

"Penn is stubborn, likes to spar with her co-workers like a UFC fighter, doesn't take well to criticism, and says whatever is on her mind."

She'd shown them all that before she left Hawaii, and

she was done hiding from them. But hearing this was for her, not them.

"She can be a little wild. Might drink a little too much before noon. And is intimate with every profane word ever in existence."

Her face flushed, and she covered it with her hand.

"But here's the thing…" Cole stopped just in front of her and let out a heavy breath. "I'd never ask her to change."

Her head shot up.

"Penn is also hot." He lifted his hand and tucked a strand of hair behind her ear. "Sexy. And one hell of a kisser."

Her entire body was reacting to his words. To the expression on his face. Her heart pounded triple time against her chest. Blood rushed through her ears, muffling the sounds going on around her, including his voice. She swallowed hard. Unable to get down the lump that had lodged into her throat. The nervous lump. The what-the-fuck-is-happening-right-now lump.

She opened her mouth to speak, but nothing came out.

"Ladies and gentlemen, I think for the very first time Penn Foster is speechless." He smiled. "A quiet Penn is a nice change." He lowered his head, but his eyes remained fixed on her as he peeked up in nervousness. "Makes it easier for me to say things like I love you."

She sucked in a breath and shook her head. She definitely was hearing things.

"I don't want to spend another day not telling you how I feel. I love you, Pennelope. I think I've loved you since the first day I met you. I just didn't know the feeling, but you woke me up. You made me believe that all of this—family, love, happiness—could happen for me."

Her head spun. This was exactly what she'd wanted to hear in Hawaii. He'd had his opportunity to say these things to her in private. Without both of their families watching and listening.

She'd already told her family that she loved Cole. That their acceptance was expected. But she hadn't told him that yet.

She planted her fists on her hips and stared him down. He couldn't just waltz in here and whisper sweet nothings. This grand sweeping gesture wasn't going to make up for the fact that he had broken her heart and left her.

"Can you also say that you're an asshole?"

Cathy gasped in shock behind her. Jack was the one who let out a laugh.

"Yes, I will also admit that I am, in fact, an asshole." He cleared his throat, and the sound echoed through the room. "But this asshole knows he made a mistake. Does that count for anything?"

She shrugged. Hitting him back with his own signature move.

"Penn, look at me," he commanded. It sent a shiver up her spine. It was the same voice he used in the bedroom. The same voice that had perfected the art of dirty talk. He grinned when she turned and looked into his eyes. No doubt he saw the desire flaring up.

"I've spent my entire life searching for happiness. And it's been right under my nose for three years. I was just too stubborn to notice."

Tears stung her eyes. But she bit them back. He couldn't do this to her. He couldn't give up and then expect her to jump back into his arms whenever he commanded.

He stood there, vulnerability in his eyes, just waiting for her to answer. He'd fucked up. Big time. But he was here. In the spotlight, something he despised, all to win her back. How could she say no to that?

"To make sure you know how serious I am, I brought reinforcements."

He picked up a bag that sat on the kitchen island and pulled out a…trophy. One that looked exactly like the Foster Cup, but it was brand new.

He held it out. The gold-plated cup sparkled in the low light of the restaurant. The dark wood stand was pristine and it had two gold plates—a large one on the bottom with swirly lettering that read "Madewood Cup" and a smaller one near the top of the wood where her name and the date was etched in the same lettering.

"I'd like to present the very first Madewood Cup to Pennelope Foster." He held out the trophy, and it sparkled in the light. "I might not have been able to help you win your family cup, but you deserve everything you want in this world. And if I have to sing karaoke or beat Finn in a game of H.O.R.S.E for you to get it, I will."

She was pretty sure at that moment her heart melted. How could she say no to him? She didn't want to say no.

"You got me a cup?"

She reached out and touched it, the smooth wood, the shiny plate. It was the greatest gift she'd ever received. But…

"I didn't do anything to deserve it." Her forehead crinkled when she looked up at him in confusion.

"That couldn't be further from the truth." He walked closer, his eyes darting up to scan the crowd that was gathered behind them. "You've spent the last three years kicking our butts into gear. Not to mention putting up with my—"

"Mood swings," Jack yelled.

"General assholishness," Neil added.

Penn giggled when she looked over her shoulder at Cole's brothers, who were totally loving this scene. For the one who was always on the sidelines and out of the spotlight, he was putting himself out there in the biggest way.

"I always thought I deserved a medal having to endure your ups and downs." She winked and reached out to grab the cup from his hand. "But a cup will totally do." She held it to her chest and squeezed it tight.

So this was what it felt like to be a winner. She looked up, right into Cole's beautiful eyes, eyes that told her everything. He had made this possible. It was because of him that she knew what it felt like to win.

He looked up and over her shoulder, his eyes surveying the crowd behind them. With a deep breath, he took her by the hand and guided her to the back of the restaurant, but not before giving Sterling a nod of his head. Weird.

When they were tucked inside his office, he shut the door behind them.

They were completely alone.

He took the cup out of her hand and placed it on the floor. He crowded her against the wall by the door, bracketing her body between his thick forearms. "No one can say you don't deserve a promotion, and no one can say it had anything to do with the way we feel about each other."

What others thought wasn't so important to her anymore. What she knew about herself, and what she had with Cole, was worth more than all that. She shook her head, focusing on the picture of the Toronto Maple Leafs logo hanging on the wall above his desk. "I can't let you resign. How is that fair?"

He tipped her chin up with one finger, forcing her to look at him. "I can still help people without being on the board."

This was everything she'd ever wanted, but now that it might be the reality of her life, it was all too much.

"How do I know you're not going to pull away again?"

"I know I have a lot to make up for." His lips grazed her forehead, and she gasped in response. She'd never get used to his touch. "I know I have a lot to prove. But…just give me a chance."

Her phone buzzed inside her dress pocket.

He pulled away, and with a small smile, he said, "You should check that out."

"Wha…" Her body tensed. They were in the middle of the most intimate conversation they'd ever had, basically making the decision of whether to become a couple, and he wanted her to look at her phone. "Why is that important?"

He reached into the tiny side pocket of her dress and grabbed the phone. Swiping the screen, he woke it up, then made a few clicks.

When he held it out to her, the *Toronto Gossip* site logo flashed at her.

Her stomach clenched. "Cole, I didn't have anything to do with more gossip about us. I swear."

"I know." His index finger swiped across her cheek in a gentle caress. "I did."

Her breath hitched. The look in his eyes was happy, playful. Devoid of the anger he'd had that night at the gym when he'd changed her world forever.

She reached out and trailed her finger up the screen, revealing the headline.

IT'S OFFICIAL: COLE MURPHY IS TAKEN!

Her jaw dropped. It was an article about them.

"Are you sure about this? With people wanting to know things about you…us?"

She knew how much he valued his privacy, and now that she knew the truth about his past it all made sense. She wouldn't do anything to jeopardize that.

"I've spent a long time living in the background, afraid that someone would find out about my past." He paused, then opened his mouth again, but no words came out. When she looked into his eyes, they were rimmed red. "Let people talk. I care more about losing a future with you than I do about my past being in the spotlight."

Shaking her head, she wrapped her arms around his neck. "I love you, Cole. So, so, so much." She couldn't hold back the tears any longer. They were now streaming down her face.

He kissed her. Soft and sweet. Full of promise. Full of exactly what she'd wanted. Cole. In her arms. Forever.

"I love you, too." He pressed his thumb to her lips and caressed them in the most intimate of gestures. "So what do we do now?"

He had turned out to be the man she'd always wanted, with the ability to give her everything she needed.

"Talk dirty to me, Murphy." She kissed him softly. "And don't ever stop."

Acknowledgments

It is with excitement and sadness that I write this acknowledgment. *Recipe for Temptation* is the last book in the Madewood Brothers series, and it seems like just yesterday I released Jack and Sterling into the world.

Thank you readers for loving the brothers just as much as I do. This series would not have been as meaningful or successful without your support and kind words. My only wish is that I can give at least one of you that contented sigh as you swipe the last page on your ereader.

Thank you to my husband, who listens to my rants even though sometimes he truly has no idea what I'm talking about. And for the last time, I will never kill off the hero at the end of a book.

Dad, thank you for believing in me, for being invested in my career, and pimping out my books to your friends' wives. But truly, Dad…stop reading my books!

Thank you Stacey Kennedy, a.k.a. the most positive

person I've ever met. Thank you for listening to my rants—even when there are more curse words than not.

Thank you Debra Kayn, who is always there when I need a shoulder to cry on...or to keep me in line.

Thank you Shana Gray, who is always there with a level head and helping me with my game plan.

Thank you Lindsay Below, my constant cheerleader and truly the wind beneath my wings.

And lastly, but definitely not least, thank you Kate Brauning. I couldn't have done this without you.

About the Author

Gina, a self-proclaimed happily ever after junkie and cupcake connoisseuse, loves spinning contemporary tales of knee bending first kisses, unconditional love and super-hot sex.

When not chained to her computer, you can find Gina sipping Starbucks, making cupcakes or feeding her addiction to celebrity gossip. She lives in Milton, Ontario with her husband and lovable dog.

www.ginagordon.net